SEASIDE
SPECTRES

D1495352

Also by Daniel W. Barefoot

SEASIDE
SPECTRES

DANIEL W. BAREFOOT

JOHN F. BLAIR, PUBLISHER

WINSTON-SALEM, NORTH CAROLINA

Published by John F. Blair, Publisher

*The paper in this book meets the guidelines
for permanence and durability of the
Committee on Production Guidelines*

*Cover photograph of Cape Hatteras Lighthouse courtesy of
North Carolina Division of Tourism, Film and Sports Development
Map courtesy of
North Carolina Department of Transportation
Design by Debra Long Hampton*

Library of Congress Cataloging-in-Publication Data
Barefoot, Daniel W., 1951–
Seaside spectres : North Carolina's haunted hundred / by Daniel W. Barefoot.
p.   cm.
ISBN 0-89587-257-9 (alk. paper)
1. Ghosts—North Carolina. 2. Haunted places—North Carolina. 3. Apparitions—North Carolina. I. Title.
BF1472.U6 B365 2002
133.1'09756—dc21
2002002799

To the memory of my father,
Pressly W. Barefoot,
who gave me family roots
on the North Carolina coast

Contents

Preface

Mists gather here, and sea fog, and eerie stories. That's not because there are more ghosts here than in other places, mind you. It's just that people who live hereabouts are strangely aware of them.

Dorothy Macardle

Steeped in history and graced with incomparable natural beauty, the North Carolina coast is known the world over as a premier vacation destination. My love affair with coastal North Carolina began with a family vacation to Wrightsville Beach in 1956, when I was five years old. Although rampant development has drastically changed the coast since my childhood visit to New Hanover County almost a half-century ago, my fascination with the region has continued to grow. Consequently, family and friends were not surprised when my first two published titles were travel/history books about the North Carolina coast.

Like me, most people who have visited or read about coastal North Carolina are enchanted by the supernatural tales, ghost stories, and unusual occurrences that have given the region much of its unique allure.

As a child growing up in North Carolina in the 1950s and

1960s, I delighted in watching Rod Serling's *The Twilight Zone* television series and the great science-fiction films of that period. At the same time, I read with great interest the classic ghost stories of North Carolina, as documented by John Harden in *The Devil's Tramping Ground* (1949) and *Tar Heel Ghosts* (1954) and by Nancy Roberts in *An Illustrated Guide to Ghosts & Other Mysterious Occurrences in the Old North State* (1959) and *Ghosts of the Carolinas* (1962).

Meanwhile, I was developing an abiding interest in the magnificent history of North Carolina. The history of the state—indeed, the history of British America—began on the soil of North Carolina with Sir Walter Raleigh's colonization attempts, which resulted in the Lost Colony of Roanoke in the 1580s. Ironically, our history as Tar Heels began with a haunting mystery that remains unresolved to this day.

When the European traditions of ghosts, witches, demons, and the like were brought to America, they landed on the shores of North Carolina. And it was on our soil that settlers documented some of the first encounters with the supernatural in America. But long before the arrival of European settlers, North Carolina was the domain of various Indian peoples. Theirs is a history replete with tales of the supernatural.

Because North Carolina has been a significant part of the American experience from the very beginning, it has emerged as one of the most historic places in the United States. And where there is history, ghosts and other elements of the supernatural can usually be found. As a longtime student of the Old North State, I can assure readers that North Carolina has a haunted heritage, one rich in the supernatural.

This book and its companion volumes offer a view of that ghostly history in a format never before presented. Here, for the first time, readers are offered a supernatural tale from each of the state's one hundred counties. But the *North Carolina's Haunted*

Hundred series is not simply a collection of Tar Heel ghost stories from every county in the state. Rather, it is a sampler of the diverse supernatural history of North Carolina. The three volumes contain accounts of ghosts and apparitions (human, animal, and inanimate), witches, strange creatures, demons, spook lights, haunting mysteries, unidentified flying objects, unexplained phenomena, and more.

Instead of retelling the timeless ghost stories so well chronicled by Harden, Roberts, Fred T. Morgan, F. Roy Johnson, Judge Charles Harry Whedbee, and others, I have chosen to present many tales that have never been widely circulated in print. I include a few of the familiar tales of our ghostly lore in the mix, but with new information or a new twist.

Do you believe in ghosts and creatures of the night? Whether your answer is yes or no, almost everyone enjoys a ghost story or an inexplicable tale of the unusual. And when that narrative has as its basis real people, actual places, and recorded events, it becomes more enjoyable because it hints at credibility and believability.

All of the stories set forth in this three-volume series are based in fact. But over the years, these tales have been told and retold, and the details have in some cases become blurred. As with all folklore, whether you choose to believe any or all of the accounts in these pages is entirely up to you. A caveat that Mark Twain once offered his readers holds true here: "I will set down a tale. . . . It may be only a legend, a tradition. It may have happened, it may not have happened. But it could have happened."

Should you develop a desire to visit some of the haunted places detailed in this series, be mindful that most are located on private property. Be sure to obtain permission from the owner before attempting to go upon any site.

From Currituck County on the Virginia border to Brunswick County on the South Carolina line, the long, irregular North

Carolina coast stretches more than three hundred miles. And beyond its Atlantic shores, the coastal plain sweeps inland for more than a hundred miles. With a tempestuous sea, winding coastal rivers and creeks, drifting sand dunes, remote islands, forbidding swamps, vast peat bogs, and stately trees draped with Spanish moss providing settings for the macabre, coastal North Carolina is home to a spooky collection of sinister beings, weird happenings, and frightening haunts. These seaside spectres now await your acquaintance, if you dare.

Acknowledgments

Writing a three-volume work with subject matter from each of the one hundred counties of North Carolina has given me a much deeper appreciation for the vastness of the state. To complete a project of this size and scope, I needed the assistance and kindly offices of innumerable people and many institutions. To all of them, I am truly grateful. There are, however, individuals who deserve special mention for their efforts on my behalf.

Extensive research was essential for the successful completion of this project. Librarians and their assistants at numerous county and municipal libraries throughout the state helped in that task by searching for materials, offering advice, and extending other courtesies to me. Pat Harden of the Norris Public Library in Rutherfordton; Chris Bates, the curator of the Carolina Room at the Public Library of Charlotte-Mecklenburg County; and Fred Turner of the Olivia Raney Local History Library in Raleigh were particularly helpful. At the reference section in the State Library of North Carolina and in the search room of the North Carolina State Archives, I always received prompt and courteous attention and assistance. At the University of North Carolina at Chapel Hill, Bob Anthony and his staff at the North

Carolina Collection and the staff at the Southern Historical Collection rendered the same outstanding assistance as they did on my prior books. At other academic libraries in the state, including those at Duke University, East Carolina University, and Appalachian State University, the special-collections personnel helped to point me in the right direction in my quest for information.

This project represents the fifth time around for me in working with Carolyn Sakowski and the excellent staff at John F. Blair, Publisher. Carolyn saw the merit in my proposal from the outset, and she was instrumental in its evolution into a three-book set. As in each of my past efforts, Steve Kirk has gone beyond the call of duty to provide his expertise as my editor. His patience, good and timely advice, keen insight, and knowledge of many subjects are deeply appreciated, and his hard work has added immeasurably to the quality of this book. Debbie Hampton, Anne Waters, Ed Southern, and all of the others at Blair are a pleasure to work with in production, publicity, and marketing.

When I issued a request for "good" ghost stories, my colleagues in the North Carolina General Assembly came to the aid of the person they refer to as their "resident historian." Special assistance was provided by Representative Bill Hurley of Fayetteville, Representative Phil Haire of Sylva, Representative Wayne Goodwin of Hamlet, and Representative Leslie Cox of Sanford.

Friends from far and wide provided support for my efforts. At the University of North Carolina at Wilmington, my friend and fellow author Dr. Chris Fonvielle offered advice and encouragement. In my hometown of Lincolnton, my friends often greeted me with a common question: "What are you writing now, Dan?" When I responded with details about *North Carolina's Haunted Hundred*, they were universally enthusiastic about the series. My crosstown friend, George Fawcett, considered by many to be the foremost authority on unidentified flying objects in North Carolina, welcomed the opportunity to provide from his vast files materials on a credible UFO landing on Tar Heel soil. Darrell Harkey, the Lincoln County historical coordinator, provided words of encouragement and friendship when they were needed most.

For its unending assistance, support, and love, I owe my family an enormous debt of gratitude I can never repay. Because of my family roots, I hold a close kinship with each of the three geographic regions in the *Haunted Hundred* set. In the 1920s, my paternal grandparents left their home in Columbus County on the coast to settle in Gaston County. About the same time, my maternal grandparents left their home in western North Carolina to put down roots in Gaston. In that Piedmont county, east thus met west, and my parents married and reared a son there.

My late father introduced me to the intriguing world of ghosts and the supernatural by taking me to those now-campy horror films of the late fifties and early sixties. My mother taught me the love of reading and writing at an early age. Both parents instilled in me a love of my native state.

My sister remains an ardent supporter of my career as a writer and historian.

My daughter, Kristie, has literally grown up while I have written eight books over the past seven years. With forbearance and love, she has endured the travels and travails of a father who has attempted to balance a career in law, politics, and history with a normal family life. Now a junior at the University of North Carolina at Chapel Hill, she has somehow found time in her extremely busy schedule to type portions of my handwritten manuscripts.

No one deserves more praise and credit for this book and all my others than my wife and best friend, Kay. It was Kay who encouraged me to combine my interests in North Carolina history and the supernatural heritage of our state to produce this book and its companion volumes. As with my previous books, Kay has meticulously read and reread every word and has acted as my sounding board for sentence structure and vocabulary. But more than that, her smiling face, her praise for me even when it's not merited, her willingness to support my every endeavor and to proudly stand beside me, her genuine kindness and unique grace, and her boundless love and constant companionship for more than twenty-seven years have blessed my life with a measure of happiness that few men ever have the good fortune to enjoy.

SEASIDE
SPECTRES

The Cursed Town

The devil hath power to assume a pleasing shape.

William Shakespeare

Today, she rests on the quiet waters of Bath and Back Creeks, much as she has for the last three hundred years. Bath, the oldest town in an old state, was incorporated by the Colonial Assembly on March 8, 1705. Homes and other structures of antiquity, including the oldest extant church in North Carolina, line the historic lanes as reminders of the time long ago when Bath was one of the most important towns in the colony. For much of the first half of the eighteenth century, it served as the unofficial capital of North Carolina and played host to several sessions of the Colonial Assembly. By the Revolutionary War, however, Bath had lost its place of dominance. And ever since, the first Tar Heel town has languished in relative obscurity.

Why Bath fell into a state of lethargy before the nineteenth century has been debated by historians through the years. Some people contend that the town was relegated to its status as a small, politically insignificant backwater hamlet by one of the most famous early evangelists in America, who put a curse on it. And perhaps it was this curse that caused Bath to have a brush with the supernatural in the early nineteenth century and made it the setting of one of the most haunting of all North Carolina legends.

Because of its location on the post road, which extended from Portland, Maine, to Savannah, Georgia, Bath attracted a wide variety of travelers and adventurers in the mid-eighteenth century. Local taverns soon acquired a reputation for bawdy and salacious activities. About the same time, colonial America was undergoing a religious experience known as the Great Awakening.

In the midst of this spiritual revival, George Whitefield, a noted English religious reformer and preacher, paid a visit to Bath on four occasions. He used his gift of oratory to condemn the vices of cursing, drinking, and dancing and to declare them the work of the devil. His fire-and-damnation sermons were not well received by the local residents, who were quite suspicious of the strange man, and for good reason.

On each visit, Whitefield brought a coffin in his wagon. When questioned about the peculiar practice, he offered a simple response: he wanted to make sure that if he died, a coffin would be waiting for his body. Folks in Bath were mortified to discover that the preacher slept in the coffin. But as he saw it, the practice allowed him to avoid the debauchery of the local inn.

In 1765, when he made what turned out to be his last visit to Bath, Whitefield received a rather cool reception and was informed that he could no longer preach in the town. Disgusted by the attitude of the citizens, the fiery minister returned to his wagon, removed his shoes, and shook the dust of Bath off them. As he drove away for the last time, Whitefield pronounced his infamous curse on the village: "There's a place in the Bible that says if a place won't listen to the Word, you shake the dust of the town off your feet, and the town shall be cursed. I have put a curse on the town for a hundred years."

Although Bath lost its political clout and did not grow during the first half of the century-long curse, no sinister evil manifested itself until an autumn day in the second decade of the nineteenth century. It has been suggested that the devil himself visited the accursed place on that occasion as a result of Whitefield's malediction.

On Sunday morning, October 13, 1813, Jesse Elliott, a local horse-racing enthusiast, was preparing for a big race to take place near Bath the following day. Elliott was a vile, profane man who wasn't above imbibing whiskey while the local churches held their worship services. As he strolled the Bath waterfront, bottle in hand, he came face to face with a nattily attired stranger—some say he was named Buckingame—atop a magnificent, shiny black horse. Pointing to Elliott's splendid chestnut, which was known to be superior to any local horse, the stranger taunted Jesse by betting a hundred dollars that the stallion could be beaten. Never one to turn his back on a challenge, Elliott quickly accepted the bet. "I'll meet you at the track in an hour," he said.

Elliott hastened home, where he promptly consumed two more glasses of liquor while donning his riding boots. His long-suffering wife pleaded with him to avoid violating the local prohibition against racing on the Sabbath. He responded with vulgarities and physical abuse. As he ambled out of the house, Mrs. Elliott tearfully screamed, "I hope you'll be sent to hell this very day!"

En route to the track, which was located on the outskirts of Bath, Elliott passed local folks as they were going home from church. They stared in disbelief and contempt, as it was obvious where the crude and callous man was headed.

When he arrived at the track, he immediately observed that

the stranger had a different look about him. His nose and ears were pointed in a way that Elliott had not noticed earlier. His dark, piercing eyes stared into Elliott's as the two men rode up to the starting line.

Suddenly, they were off! As the two fleet thoroughbreds galloped around the course, Elliott was delighted to hold his own against the strange challenger. Encouraged that he could win the race and the wager, he prodded his animal as if he were possessed. "Take me in a winner or take me to hell!" he cried.

His command had its intended effect on the horse, as Elliott soon found himself in the lead. For some reason, however, the stranger appeared unconcerned about the growing distance between the two steeds. Eyewitnesses claimed they even heard him offer a soft, diabolical laugh.

Elliott could sense victory as he neared the final turn toward the homestretch. But in the curve, his horse twisted its head and whinnied in terror. The unfortunate animal had caught a glimpse of what was pursuing it: the devil riding a black horse. It stopped suddenly, dug its hooves into the soft dirt, and powerfully expelled its rider. Jesse Elliott was sent flying headfirst into a nearby pine tree. He died instantly.

Bystanders claim that Buckingame—or the devil, if you will—did not slow down for the accident. Instead, he just galloped off into the woods and on to hell, to join Jesse Elliott there.

As far as anyone knows, the devil was never seen around Bath again. Perhaps Whitefield's words finally took root after that Sunday in 1813, for local ministers began to preach against the evils of gambling and drinking. As they saw it, the tragedy that had befallen Elliott was an example of the fate awaiting those who engaged in such iniquity.

For months after the accident, Elliott's hair could be seen hanging from the tree where he had met his demise. Over time, that side of the tree turned brown, while the other side remained green and healthy. Finally, the old pine died and was reduced to nothing more than a stump.

Today, there are lasting reminders of the day the devil visited the place cursed by Whitefield. To see the site where Jesse Elliott's horse screeched to a halt on the racetrack almost two hundred years ago, drive west from Bath on NC 92 for two and a half miles to the junction with SR 1334. Turn left and proceed a mile or so to a pull-off on the east shoulder of SR 1334. Near a wooded area approximately a quarter-mile from the road are eight distinct but very mysterious hoof prints that have captivated the interest of Tar Heels since the early nineteenth century. Because this unmarked site is located on private property, be sure to obtain permission from the owner before visiting.

The saucer-shaped depressions on the old Cutlar farm have remained unchanged since Jesse Elliott's horse reportedly made them in 1813. That they have survived for so long is remarkable, considering that countless efforts have been made to eradicate or alter them. No vegetation grows in the holes. Numerous people have attempted to fill them with all kinds of debris. On their way to school, children have put trash in the indentations, only to find that the holes are empty by day's end. Although a lush carpet of pine needles completely surrounds the site, none of the needles ever finds a permanent resting place in the hoof prints. When the farm's chickens were fed, grain was often scattered into the holes. The birds would peck around the hoof prints but not inside. When the owner decided to use it for a pigsty, the swine refused to eat any food that fell into the impressions. In short order, the hogs reduced the hoof prints to a muddy ooze. Incredibly, once the animals were removed, the unusual depressions reappeared exactly where they had been.

Several scientific investigations have been conducted in an attempt to solve the mystery surrounding the hoof prints. Duke

University and the American Society of Psychical Research combined resources to study the phenomenon. Their equipment, specially designed to detect psychokinetic forces, provided no answers. In the course of the experiments, the impressions were filled with trash and secured with thread. While the scientists were away from the site, the debris disappeared from the holes.

Many theories have been espoused to explain the mysterious hoof prints of Bath. One of the most popular is that they are the result of underground salt veins or pockets of water.

By the middle of the twentieth century, four to five thousand visitors were coming annually to see the site.

Did George Whitefield's curse on Bath work? For an answer, you need only look at the ancient town, which is not much larger now than it was almost three centuries ago. Then take a look at the strange hoof prints. Who can argue that they aren't tangible evidence of one man's journey to hell for the very vices Whitefield decried?

A Shrew Untamed

Don't let us make imaginary evils, when you know we have so many real ones to encounter.

Oliver Goldsmith

Established in 1722, Bertie County is one of the oldest political subdivisions in North Carolina. One of the most venerable family names in Bertie is Castellaw (spelled alternately as Castelloe, Castellow, and Castello). James Castellaw brought the name to this part of North Carolina when he immigrated from Scotland in the first half of the eighteenth century. From his arrival in Bertie, the young merchant and planter was a political leader. It was upon his land that the first county courthouse was built.

The Castellaw name has survived into modern times. In the middle of the twentieth century, one of Bertie's most historic homes, Windsor Castle, was restored to its former glory by Dr. Cola Castelloe. And Castelloe Road, located six miles east of the county seat of Windsor, pays homage to this old family name of Bertie.

There is one member of the Castellaw family who refused

to rest after her death. Her ghost is the basis of this chilling tale, which unfolded about the same time the Civil War engulfed America. In 1862, John Castellaw, his wife, and their three children lived on a small farm located about three miles east of Windsor at a place known as Turkey Swamp. Their log cabin, set amid the vast pocosins of eastern Bertie, was not a place of domestic tranquility. John Castellaw and his ill-tempered wife, a shrew of a woman, did not get along. They argued and berated each other almost constantly.

As to their children, Mr. and Mrs. Castellaw openly picked favorites. Milly was the apple of John's eye, so his wife chose Mary, the other daughter. David, the third child, elected to avoid the strife at home by volunteering to fight for the Confederate army. But before he left Bertie County, he gave a large sum of money to his mother, who promptly buried it on the farm.

While David was away at war, things went from bad to worse at the Castellaw home. His mother's health deteriorated. As death drew near for the hateful wretch, she uttered a stern warning to Mary: "If you stay here with the old man and Milly after I'm dead and gone, I'll come back and pull your eyes out."

Soon thereafter, Mrs. Castellaw passed away. Her corpse was buried near the family cabin. But she did not rest there for long. One night as John, Mary, and Milly were sitting about the cabin, there came a loud knock at the door. John answered it but found no one there. Over the next several nights, the family continued to hear the same mysterious sounds.

Living in the wilds of Bertie County, John Castellaw was not a man who was easily frightened. But as spring gave way to summer, his courage was challenged, for "the Thing"—as he and the girls called it—became more aggressive. While they were in bed, the unseen visitor would cover their faces with quilts and blankets. Then it would take their pillows and pummel them.

The disturbances became a nightly occurrence, and the terrified family members found they could not sleep. When they tried to steal some slumber during daylight, "the Damned Booger"—as the highly annoyed John was then calling it—began to make its presence known during those hours also.

On one occasion, a broadax was observed moving in a menacing manner about the farmyard without anyone visibly controlling it. More than once, while the Castellaws were assembled at the dining table, a half-brick or similar heavy object would fall suddenly from the joist above, making a deep impression in the table. At least a half-dozen times, the Thing threw an apple at Mary's head.

There was no end to the violent outbursts by the vindictive haunt. After a long day of hard labor on the farm, John walked into the yard to enjoy the cool of the evening following supper. As he rested under a cedar tree, the Damned Booger knocked his hat off. Outraged, he exclaimed, "Damn you, knock it off! I can put it on as many times as you can knock it off, I reckon." No sooner had he taken his seat than the haunt grabbed his hair and pulled some of it out. Neighbors were invited to spend the night with the Castellaws in order to give them support when the Thing made its nightly call. These visitors invariably departed the farm in a state of shock and fear after witnessing the sights and sounds that plagued John and his family.

Meanwhile, David Castellaw had deserted from the Confederate army and enlisted in the Union army. When his military duties were over, he returned to the family farm, where the horrifying occurrences continued. Before David died in November 1867, he shot at the Thing several times. Although he was extremely reluctant to discuss his frightening experiences with the ghost, the young man confirmed before his premature death what other family members had suspected. The Thing was his mother. He had seen it!

Sometime after David died, John and the girls fled the

haunted place. They settled on a farm a mile or so from Windsor. As far as anyone knows, the Thing did not follow them and never made good on its threat to pull Mary's eyes out. At their new homestead, the family lived in relative peace.

But what about the old Castellaw farm? A man by the name of Simpson purchased the property. Some say that he found the money and other valuables buried there by Mrs. Castellaw. Others are not so sure because they say her ghost would not allow the treasure to be taken. Indeed, folks in these parts claim that the grave near the old cabin site at Turkey Creek remains empty and that the Damned Booger still haunts the Bertie countryside.

Phantom Flames

When every fact, every present or past phenomenon of the universe, every phase of present or past life therein has been examined . . . then the mission of science will be completed.

Karl Pearson

Established in 1734, Bladen County once stretched to the western limits of British America. Its nickname, "Mother of Counties," is well deserved, as fifty-five of North Carolina's counties were carved from land that was once Bladen. It is little wonder, then, that a place so steeped in history and tradition is the site of numerous eerie occurrences. Ironically, the county was almost two hundred years old when it became the site of a famous case of the mysterious phenomenon known as spontaneous combustion.

For many years, scientists have tried in vain to explain why objects burst into flames without the application of an external heat source. Documented reports of spontaneous human combustion date back to the second half of the seventeenth century.

Because most of the early cases involved corpulent elderly female alcoholics who burned near open fireplaces, their unfortunate deaths were attributed to the divine intervention of God as punishment for their vices.

About the time that Bladen County was created, the first scholarly report of spontaneous combustion was written in Italy. Over the next hundred years, numerous reports of the phenomenon circulated in America and Europe. By the middle of the nineteenth century, the anomaly was so well known that Charles Dickens used it to kill a fictional character called Krook in his novel *Bleak House*.

Dickens's book caused a minor uproar in the scientific community. Some scholars criticized the British author for popularizing what they deemed to be nothing more than a superstition. Responding to the criticism, Dickens noted in the preface to the second edition of the novel that he had carefully studied some thirty reports of spontaneous combustion.

During the eighty years that followed the publication of *Bleak House*, there were more than a half-dozen credible cases around the world. But it was on a chilly January morning in 1932 in Bladenboro, the seat of Bladen County, that one of the most widely reported incidents occurred. On that day, Mrs. Charles Williamson, a housewife, was going about her daily routine when the cotton dress she was wearing suddenly burst into flames. At the time of the fire, Mrs. Williamson was neither smoking nor standing near a fireplace or any other source of flame or heat. Her dress had not been exposed to any substance that could have caused combustion.

Responding quickly, her husband and teenage daughter ripped the flaming garment from her body with their bare hands. Miraculously, neither the victim nor the rescuers suffered a single burn, although Mrs. Williamson's frock was reduced to little more than a charred rag.

Later that same day, the mysterious fire returned when a pair of trousers belonging to Mr. Williamson burst into flames while hanging in a closet.

After spending an uneasy but uneventful night, the Williamson family was in the company of friends the next day when horrifying events began once again in the house. In an unoccupied bedroom, a bed unaccountably caught fire. By the time the blaze was extinguished, the bed coverings had been completely consumed. Then the curtains in the same room burst into flames.

For the next three days, strange fires in the home destroyed numerous articles that were not exposed in any way to a source of heat or flame. Mysteriously, the fires did not spread to nearby flammable objects. Rather, they burned out after incinerating the specific items they had attacked.

Among the reliable witnesses who observed the odd events at the Williamson home were J. A. Bridger, the mayor of Bladenboro; J. B. Edwards, a public-health officer from Wilmington; and Dr. S. S. Hutchinson, the Williamson family's physician. They described bluish flames that destroyed objects without changing color. According to an Associated Press report, the fires produced no smoke and very little odor.

After four days of terror, the Williamsons could take it no more and moved out. In the wake of their departure, law enforcement and fire officials scoured the house in an unsuccessful effort to locate liquids or materials that might have caused the fires. Electricians found no problems with the wiring. Workers from the gas company confirmed that there were no leaks in the residence. Nonetheless, the blue flames continued to ignite while the officials inspected the dwelling.

Finally, the fires disappeared after playing havoc for five days. The family moved back home and was never again troubled by the phenomenon. Fortunately, no human was injured by the sudden fires in this small town in southeastern North Carolina.

To this day, the odd events that took place in Bladenboro in 1932 are cited as one of the best examples of the curious phenomenon known as spontaneous combustion. And after all the years that have elapsed, the words in the old Associated Press report provide a haunting summary of this great mystery of Bladen: "The fires started, burned out and vanished as mysteriously as if guided by invisible hands. There has been no logical explanation."

The Cape of Fear

There it stands today, bleak and threatening, and piti-less. . . . And its nature, its name, is now, always has been, and always will be the Cape of Fear.

George Davis

Cape Fear, the southernmost of North Carolina's three capes, is located at the tip of Bald Head Island in Brunswick County. Although the cape was so named because of the treach-erous shoals that lie just offshore in the Atlantic, it has long been the home of ghosts that have stricken fear in the many people who have encountered them.

Bald Head Island is a spectacular collage of beaches, dunes, maritime forests, freshwater ponds, estuaries, and mud flats. While some parts of the island have been developed as a luxury resort, a significant portion of Bald Head, including beautiful maritime forests, has been left in its natural state. Teeming with unusual plants and animals, the ancient island forests are unlike any others in North Carolina. Growing among the pines and live oaks are Sabal palmettos. These palm trees, living evidence of the semitropical climate of the island, grow naturally nowhere else in North Carolina.

It was a Bald Head Island forest that provided the setting for one of the greatest unsolved mysteries in North Carolina history: the disappearance of Theodosia Burr Alston. This intriguing story remains a part of the lore of two distinct areas of the state's coast: the Outer Banks and Bald Head Island.

While several places claim to be the site of the mystery, there are certain indisputable facts related to the story. Theodosia Burr Alston was the wife of Joseph Alston, the governor of South Carolina, and the daughter of Aaron Burr, the third vice president of the United States. She was known as a woman of striking beauty, intelligence, and sophistication. On the last day of 1812, she is said to have boarded a small ship, *The Patriot*, at Georgetown, South Carolina, for a trip to New York for a reunion with her father, who had recently returned from self-imposed exile in England after his famous duel with Alexander Hamilton. Whether because of a storm or piracy, *The Patriot* never arrived in New York. Rather, it drifted ashore at Nags Head in early 1813, devoid of passengers and crew.

At this point, the theories about Theodosia's disappearance diverge. Some evidence suggests that pirates killed her and plundered *The Patriot* while the ship was off Nags Head. On the other hand, some historians have suggested that the ship was stranded on the shoals of Cape Fear. As *The Patriot* foundered, the pirates of Bald Head Island moved in. After plundering the helpless vessel, the raiders threw the crew and passengers overboard, save for Theodosia, whose magnificent beauty apparently led them to spare her life. Sometime later, according to this second theory, the ransacked and abandoned vessel was set adrift by the tides, to be carried to its final resting place at Nags Head. Meanwhile, Theodosia was brought to the pirate leader in the forests of Bald

Head. He recognized her to be the first lady of South Carolina and realized her enormous ransom potential. Until arrangements could be made to contact Governor Alston for a payoff, Theodosia was placed in the custody of three pirates. They soon became intoxicated with rum, and Theodosia escaped into the night. One story says that her lifeless body was discovered in the dense forest by a search party of pirates after she committed suicide. Outraged by the incompetence of his subordinates, the pirate chieftain ordered the threesome beheaded. A divergent tale has it that the search party found Theodosia alive and returned her to the pirate camp, where she died in captivity. Yet another twist to the Bald Head story was given credibility by two men who were hanged in Norfolk after the ill-fated voyage of *The Patriot*. At their trial, the men testified that they were members of the band of pirates responsible for pillaging *The Patriot* at Bald Head. They bore witness to Theodosia's death.

Regardless of how Theodosia may have met her demise at Bald Head, various accounts of her ghost persist to this day. Before the development of the island, the apparition was seen roaming the beaches and forests in a relentless search for a way to escape. In more recent times, her ghost, attired in an elegant emerald-green dress, has been observed about the island.

Not only has the beautiful lady continued to haunt Bald Head, but so have the three pirates assigned to guard her. In the distant past, the headless ghosts were observed pursuing the ghost of poor Theodosia. When the Coast Guard manned a station on the island near Cape Fear, Guardsmen walked the beach on patrol each night. More than once, stunned sentries returned to the station with tales of headless pirates joining them on their rounds.

Many years have passed since the last Guardsmen patrolled the beaches of the island, but sightings of the headless phantoms have continued. Lovers strolling the moonlit beaches or the lonely maritime forests have been startled by ghosts, who often tap young women on the shoulder in hopes that they might be the elusive Theodosia.

Should you have the opportunity to tour or vacation on Bald Head, take heed that you might encounter the ghosts of pirates or of a glamorous young lady. For after all, you will be visiting the place long known as the Cape of Fear.

Terrors of the Swamp

By the grey woods,——by the swamp
Where the toad and the newt encamp,——
By the dismal tarns and pools
Where dwell the Ghouls . . .

Edgar Allen Poe

No place in all of North Carolina has a more sinister name than the Great Dismal Swamp. Many motorists who cross the Virginia-North Carolina border into Camden County via US 17 pass through one of the world's most famous wilderness areas without ever knowing it. Beside the roadway sprawls an almost impenetrable jungle, the northernmost link in the chain of large swamps of the mid-Atlantic coastal plain.

Drainage has reduced the Great Dismal from two thousand square miles to its present six hundred square miles. Nonetheless, the morass of cypress forests, peat bogs, lakes, and streams envelops a massive parcel of land in southeastern Virginia and northeastern North Carolina. The swamp is roughly half the size of the state of Rhode Island. There remains a popular misconception that all or most of the Great Dismal is located in Virginia. To the contrary, almost 60 percent of the existing swamp is within the North Carolina counties of Camden, Currituck, Gates, Pasquotank, and Perquimans.

Scientists estimate the age of the Great Dismal at between six thousand and nine thousand years. Once under the sea, this natural treasure emerged as a landform when the continental shelf last made a significant shift.

William Byrd, in his historic quest to survey the dividing line between Virginia and North Carolina in 1728, provided America with its first written description of this enormous wilderness: "The ground of this swamp is a mere quagmire, trembling under the feet of those who walk upon it. . . . Never was rum, that cordial of life found more necessary than in this dirty place." The Indians who lived in northeastern North Carolina and southeastern Virginia in Byrd's day maintained a healthy respect for the place. At times, their respect bordered on fear. Consequently, few of their number were willing to brave the Great Dismal after the sun went down.

Now, almost three centuries later, the swamp maintains its ominous, mysterious aura. While some of the unusual animals that once inhabited it—the American buffalo, for example—vanished long ago, a variety of dangerous beasts such as bears, wildcats, and venomous snakes and spiders thrive in this primeval tangle of vines, thick vegetation, and unstable ground.

There exist some remote portions of the Great Dismal that have never been seen by human eyes. Over the years, countless men have ventured into the swamp, never to be seen again. It is not surprising, then, that the place is the origin of many eerie legends and frightening tales. Unusual sights and bloodcurdling sounds reported from the swamp have inspired a variety of stories involving ghosts, spirits, ghouls, witches, fairies, strange creatures, fierce beasts, and other supernatural beings.

Hunters, drawn to the swamp because of its prodigious quantity of game, have sometimes gotten more than they bargained for. Take Harvey Pruitt, for example. On a hunting and trapping expedition into the Great Dismal many years ago, Pruitt encountered a horrifying creature that may well have been a Bigfoot. The legendary Bigfoot is most closely associated with the Pacific Northwest, but one of the first published reports of its existence concerned a sighting in the Balsam Mountains of western North Carolina; indeed, at least one sighting has been noted in more than fifty of the state's counties. A contemporary account of the Dismal Swamp Freak—as the creature was locally named—provided a brief physical description: "This hideous thing, almost as huge as a bear, covered with long black hair, ran on its hind feet. It resembled a bear, but I would swear on a stack of Bibles, that it could not be a bear. When Harvey chanced upon the thing and surprised it, it screamed like a panther. It ran as fast as a deer, but of course it couldn't be a deer."

As soon as the swamp monster caught sight of Pruitt, it gave chase, forcing the hunter to flee for his life through the briers and brambles. After surviving the ordeal, the intrepid outdoorsman assembled a group of fellow adventurers the following day. The heavily armed men took to the swamp to find "the most frightening varmint [Pruitt] had ever seen." Using his incomparable knowledge of the Great Dismal, Pruitt tracked down the creature, captured it, and brought it out of the wilderness alive. He confined it in a cage on his property.

News of Harvey Pruitt's amazing discovery spread quickly. People who lived on the fringes of the swamp came to behold the wonder that the Great Dismal had produced. Old-timers swore that nothing of its kind had ever been witnessed in these parts. In their bewilderment over what the beast was, someone recalled tales about escaped slaves who had reverted to a wild state after taking up refuge in the swamp. But the Dismal Swamp Freak was not one of them.

Try as he might, Harvey Pruitt could not induce the captured beast to eat the food he prepared for it. Ultimately, it wasted away and died a caged animal.

What was the Dismal Swamp Freak? Could it have been the only Bigfoot captured to date in the entire world? Are there more of its kind lurking in the vast recesses of the swamp?

Although the Dismal Swamp Freak was not a humanoid, this wilderness has done strange things to some of the people who have been fearless enough to take up residence in it. In 1912, the *Norfolk Virginian-Pilot* printed a report about a weird swamp dweller who inhabited a long, coffin-like structure. He was described thus: "The hermit who lives here is a friendly, short man with unshaven face, and unshorn mass of gray hair. He speaks an unintelligible gibberish. He was dressed in a most inconceivable assortment of cast-off clothing, each garment ingeniously patched and mended until little of the original cloth remained."

Mysterious lights have been witnessed in the Great Dismal for as long as its history has been recorded. Scientists have deemed the bluish white lights to be swamp gas. And then there are the ghosts that float about the swamp. Sir Thomas Moore, the noted Irish poet, visited the Great Dismal in 1803 while serving as consul to Bermuda. There, he heard the story of the ghost of an Indian girl who was frequently seen paddling her eerie white canoe in the waters of the swamp. Moore immortalized her ghost in his classic poem "The Lake of Dismal Swamp."

Two decades before Moore visited the Great Dismal, its wilderness was the setting for ghostly drama during the American Revolution. It was a wartime incident here that produced the phantom French voices that can still be heard in the North Carolina portion of the swamp.

In its quest to aid the American war effort, France sent troops across the Atlantic. One of its warships, laden with gold to pay the troops fighting in the colonies, was forced to seek shelter at Hampton Roads because of a savage storm. Once inside the protected waters of that Virginia harbor, the ship hastened up the Elizabeth River to avoid a confrontation with British vessels. In the process, the French ship was sighted by an enemy man-of-war, which gave chase. In the course of the pursuit, the fleeing ship was forced into shallow water. Fearing that his vessel would be grounded, the captain ordered it burned after the cargo of gold was loaded into smaller boats. On came the relentless British. The French crewmen hid the gold in the river and along its banks. They then fled deep into the Great Dismal, where their British attackers finally overtook them. In the bloody hand-to-hand combat that ensued, all the French sailors were slaughtered. To this day, their voices can still be heard echoing across the expanse.

Located on US 17 approximately three miles south of the Virginia-North Carolina border, the Great Dismal Swamp Canal Visitor Center is an excellent place for motorists to get a safe view of the historic swamp. But this is about as close as most folks should get. For, you see, lurking within the jungle nearby are known and unknown terrors that belong only in a place so aptly named the Great Dismal Swamp.

Haunted Island

*Science fiction is no more written for scientists than ghost
stories are written for ghosts.*

Brian W. Aldiss

Harbor Island, reduced by wind and tide to a mere half-
acre dot of sand in Core Sound, is a ghost of its former self.
Located in northeastern Carteret County several miles offshore
from Cedar Island, the once horseshoe-shaped island rests in the
center of a chain of three islands, the others being Wainwright's
and Chain Shot. The islands separate Core Sound from Pamlico
Sound. Shown on the Moseley map of North Carolina in 1733,
Harbor Island was once at least ten times its present size.

When waterfowl hunting came of age in the state in the last
quarter of the nineteenth century, wealthy hunters from the
North descended upon Carteret County to avail themselves of
the copious waterfowl of Core Sound. Among the famous Americans who came to hunt here were Babe Ruth and Franklin D.
Roosevelt. Harbor Island was an ideal site for the construction
of one of the many gun clubs that sprang up on the waters of the
sound.

Around 1886, John Pike, a native of New York, purchased Harbor Island. A year later, he built a hunting lodge there and formed the Harbor Island Club with fellow New Yorkers. Designed to resist the violent hurricanes and nor'easters that frequently rake the North Carolina coast, the two-and-a-half-story, ten-bedroom structure was constructed of the sturdiest of materials. Its foundation and walls were fabricated of tabby, a mixture of seashells, mortar, and sand. The floors were heart pine.

Under the administration of Lawrence Pike, the hunting lodge on Harbor Island grew in popularity and gained a ghost. A black man who was employed to perform maintenance on the clubhouse, the auxiliary buildings, and the waterfront docks arrived on the island one evening to ready the place for guests expected the following day. According to one account, the maintenance man and Pike had a heated disagreement later that night. The black man was never seen or heard from again. No other boat arrived or departed the docks that evening, and Pike was the only other person known to have been on the island.

When the boatload of guests drew close to the pier at Harbor Island the next day, they called out for assistance to tie their lines. To their dismay, the island was deserted. After the black man was discovered missing, a thorough search of the clubhouse and the surrounding landscape was conducted. But it yielded no evidence of foul play.

Folks from the Carteret County mainland began to speculate that Pike had killed him, disposed of his body, and fled the island. When he was later questioned about the unexplained disappearance, Pike responded bluntly: "Who the hell wants to know?"

Not long after the strange disappearance, Lawrence Pike sold his interest in Harbor Island and moved away. But there lingered a vestige of his tenure as an owner: the ghost of the black man. Guests who spent a night in the lodge began to report eerie noises and other supernatural happenings. They were often awakened from a deep sleep by mysterious, unexplained footsteps on the wooden floors of the clubhouse.

In 1912, a corporation known as Harbor Island Hunting Lodge acquired the island and its facilities. Among the stockholders was John Motley Morehead, a prominent benefactor of the University of North Carolina. Despite the change in ownership, the haunting persisted.

One of the most frightening encounters with the ghost took place when Jim Downing, then the only black resident of Cedar Island, arrived at the island docks one evening with the intention of spending the night. He secured his boat and stepped ashore. As he made his way toward the lodge, Downing felt a bullet whiz by his head and heard the sound of a gun. After a complete search of the island and the clubhouse, the shaken man hastily departed the island with the firm conviction that the ghost of Harbor Island was armed with a gun.

After suffering severe damage from a series of storms, the lodge underwent a complete renovation in 1937. Still, the ghost continued to make its presence known. The last hunting parties were headquartered in the clubhouse in the mid-1940s. Thereafter, the structure was abandoned to the harsh coastal elements.

Today, waves lap against all that remains of the once-grand lodge—a portion of the tabby walls and foundation. The fast-vanishing island is now home only to shrieking gulls and the spectre who represents the days of its former glory as a hunters' paradise. Fishermen who work the nearby waters have heard phantom footsteps on the shore and observed a mysterious light on certain nights. Maybe, just maybe, the restless ghost of that murdered laborer will find its body before Harbor Island completely disappears under the waters of Core Sound and is no more.

The Bewitched Miller

Better to be killed than frightened to death.

R. S. Surtees

From the annals of American folklore and tradition has evolved the stereotypical description of a witch. The word conjures up a vivid mental picture: she is an old, grotesque woman with a pronounced hooked nose with a prominent wart on it; she is attired in black or dark clothing and a tall, pointed hat; her stooped frame is stirring a large, black cauldron over a fire; and sitting nearby in the sinister setting is a black cat.

As frightening as is the classic picture, the "real" witch has been documented as an even more ominous entity because of her ability to change her physical appearance into forms ranging from a beautiful woman to a menacing black cat. Accordingly, this tale of horror from Chowan County tells of a lovely young lady, the hardworking miller who married her, a black cat, and witchcraft.

One of the most famous water mills in North Carolina was the Brownrigg Mill, the construction of which was authorized by the County Court of Chowan County in July 1762. A decade after the mill went into operation on Indian Creek, Tim Farrow was appointed as the miller in charge. A tireless and conscientious worker, Tim often remained at the mill to drop his fishing line in the dark waters after a day of hard labor. He was often observed at twilight making his way to his cottage across the dam with a string of catfish and perch.

Surrounding the millpond was a forbidding wilderness. One day, darkness was fast closing in on a pleasant afternoon of fishing when Tim looked up from the glassy waters to cautiously survey the spooky vastness all about him. He noticed a canoe making its way on to the pond from the shadow lands. Across the water it came, finally to the point where the miller could ascertain that its only occupant was a woman. Covering her head was a Shaker bonnet. From a distance, she appeared to be a rather old hag. But when the canoe pulled up to the dam, a young woman of breathtaking beauty emerged. The lady looked to be fatigued and hungry. Tim readily consented to her request for food and a place to spend the night.

The female visitor related a woeful story of distress and impoverishment. Tim was soon taken with his guest, but his attraction to her was far more than physical. Her personality, her mannerisms, her efforts to turn the cottage into a comfortable home, and her motherly tenderness for his daughter caused the middle-aged widower to fall in love with her. In but a short time, they were married.

The newlyweds had little time to settle down to a life of marital bliss, for Tim's neighbors were suspicious of his wife and perceived that there was something evil about her. Not far from the mill lived a woman with whom Tim's wife had spent a night before she met him. According to the woman, the feather bed in which the mysterious lady had slept was depressed only in a small, round spot in the center, as if a cat had lain there.

Then the residents of area farms were stricken with a strange illness that local physicians had never seen. After several persons died from the malady, there was a hue and cry that Tim's spouse was a witch.

When several neighbors paid a visit to the miller and demanded that his wife be banished from the area, Tim angrily dismissed his callers. Before long, business at the mill dropped and profits plummeted. Tim feared that his livelihood was in jeopardy. So, too, was his marriage, for his vibrant, young wife seemed to be losing interest in him.

As if these troubles were not enough, various mechanical problems and other difficulties began to manifest themselves at the mill. Water gates that Tim had closed were found partially open. Nails that mysteriously appeared in the hopper caused erratic movements of the millstones. Bear-grass thongs, used by the miller to tie the sacks of grain and meal, were found scattered about the mill when he reported for work each morning. Sacks of corn were torn open, the kernels spilled all over the floor.

Mounting anger spurred Tim to action. Indignant that his neighbors would sabotage the mill and waste its product, he decided to lie in wait at night for the culprits.

Several nights produced no intruders, other than the usual rats scurrying about in the darkness in search of food. Tim pondered what he should do next.

When a fierce thunderstorm struck close to nightfall, a strange feeling came over him that the source of his torment would return that stormy night. Consequently, he told his wife that he was going to a store some distance away and would return home very late. Instead, he hurried back to the mill, where he went into hiding behind some large bags of freshly ground meal.

His uncomfortable wait was rendered even more unpleasant

by the crashing thunder, flashing lightning, and torrential rainfall that pounded the building. Finally, the storm relented, but the sound of its fury was supplanted by a loud, eerie cacophony produced by the multitude of frogs in the millpond. For Tim, this racket was more disconcerting than the storm, because frogs were often associated with the devil and were used by witches to cast spells.

Then came more sounds and sights to add to Tim's uneasiness. Fireflies, in numbers and with a brightness Tim had never seen before, made their way into the mill and produced an odd blinking effect in the otherwise dark building. An enormous owl found a perch atop the roof and offered three horrific screeches that almost caused the miller to jump out of his skin.

Ordinarily, Tim would have thought nothing of the storm, the frogs, the fireflies, or the owl, but taken together on that frightful night, he saw them as an omen. His heart pounding rapidly, he jumped to his feet, anxious to reach the safety of his cottage. But before he could leave, there were loud knocks at the door.

"Who would come to the mill at this time of night?" Tim thought to himself. There was no opportunity to answer the knocks, because the door suddenly flew open. In sprang a mass of forty black cats. Backs arched, tails bushed out, eyes glowing, the animals encircled the miller as if they were controlled by a supernatural force. Tim could hardly believe his eyes when the ferocious felines, moving almost in unison, slowly closed the circle to the point where they could strike at him with their claws.

In his time of danger, Tim had the presence of mind to grab a nearby ax. Gripping it firmly, he raised the weapon over his head and slammed it down in the direction of an especially evil-looking old cat that had been clawing at him. The blade chopped off the right front foot of the animal. Screaming in agony, the cat hobbled out the back door, followed by the other felines.

Anxious to relate the horrifying events of the evening to his wife, Tim hurried to the cottage. But his real nightmare was just beginning. That his wife was already in bed was not unusual, because the hour was late. However, her right hand had been severed at the wrist. Speechless, Tim stood near the bed as if in a daydream. When he came to his senses, he commenced interrogating her about her missing member. No answers were forthcoming, for the woman suddenly changed into a cat and ran out of the cottage.

Tim was ready to give chase when he heard a loud roaring of water, as if a flood were bearing down on the millpond. He dashed to raise the gates in order to save the mill. When he was halfway across the dam, the structure began to shake and tremble. In an instant, more than a hundred feet of the dam were washed away by the onrushing water. Tim's night of terror came to a final, tragic end when he drowned in the deluge.

In the wake of Tim's death, the dam was repaired and a new miller was hired to operate the facility. Soon after he took charge, an old, black cat with three legs began to annoy the man as he went about his daily duties. At length, he decided to put an end to the pest. He loaded his gun with silver money, aimed it at the cat, and squeezed the trigger. Folks in that part of Chowan County were never again bothered by witches.

The Immigrant Ghost

Even the grave yawns for him!

Sir Herbert D. B. Tree

North Carolina is rightfully proud of the many home-grown ghosts that have haunted the state throughout its long and storied history. But the state also counts among its haunts the ghost of a man who came to this country from Russia in the first decade of the twentieth century.

His story is set in Bolton, a small town located in northeastern Columbus County along NC 214 and US 74 on the fringes of the vast Green Swamp. Sprawling over 140 square miles, the swamp is a mysterious, forbidding land of peat-and-muck timberland. Portions of the eerie morass were once owned by Patrick Henry. For more than a century, lumber and paper companies in the Bolton area have availed themselves of the plentiful timber resources.

Deep inside one of the seemingly boundless forests near Bolton stands a solitary marble headstone. It marks the grave of Steve Rossin, who was born in Russia in 1876. He was buried here soon after he died in his adopted Columbus County on November 6, 1936. But there are those who say that the ghost of this Russian immigrant haunts the surrounding forest.

To understand why Steve cannot rest, it is important to know something of his life. No one is absolutely sure why he left Russia to settle here. Local tradition has it that he came to North Carolina as a young man to avoid military service in the Russo-Japanese War, fought in 1904 and 1905. At any rate, soon after his arrival in Bolton, he was labeled "Steve Russian" by local folks in an obvious play on his name.

Initially, the short, stocky man with black hair and beard took up residence in the swampy wilderness that even today surrounds Bolton. There, he lived like a wild man. His shelter was nothing more than a mud-and-straw hut, and his diet consisted of wild animals, including skunks, which he hunted in the dense swamp wilderness.

Although most people found Steve to be gentle and polite, his rough appearance and lack of personal hygiene prevented him from developing many friendships. He rarely bathed, and he chose to wear a single pair of overalls until they literally fell apart.

When he first arrived, Steve worked for the railroad that passed through Bolton. Later, as his English improved, he performed odd jobs for area residents. As he grew older, he began to sleep near the boilers in the town's old mill in order to keep warm on cold winter nights.

When they arrived for work one morning, mill employees found Steve's lifeless body. He had died in his sleep. Money was collected in the community so that Steve could be provided a proper burial and a marked grave.

In the years since his death, many strange things have happened in the forest that surrounds Steve's grave. Residents of a house near the burial site have heard phantom knocks at their door. Other area residents have reported hearing eerie sounds emanating from the vicinity of Steve's grave. Many folks believe that the ghost of Steve Rossin wanders the forest in a fruitless search for the money he hid under an oak tree many, many years ago. Over time, the paper company that owns the forest has cut countless trees. It is believed that the trees Steve used for land-marks have been harvested. Sadly, the Russian ghost must scour the entire forest in his endless quest for his money.

If you pass through Bolton on a dark night, you just might hear North Carolina's immigrant ghost as he seeks the modest riches that were his in his adopted home.

Ghostly Presents

Through open doors
The harmless phantoms on their errands glide,
With feet that make no sound upon the floors.

Henry Wadsworth Longfellow

Say the word *ghost*, and most people envision a super-natural being that brings apprehension and fear to the place it haunts. The very thought of an encounter with the apparition of a dead person is disconcerting. Nonetheless, the history of ghostly spirits in North Carolina suggests that not all of these spectres are malevolent. To the contrary, some of them have proven help-ful to the humans who occupy their haunted places.

One such ghost can be found in a home in New Bern, the second-oldest city in North Carolina. Strategically laid out at the confluence of the Neuse and Trent Rivers in the first decade of the eighteenth century, New Bern emerged as the colonial and state capital from 1746 until 1792. Its original street plan, now almost three hundred years old, survives virtually intact.

Along the historic streets and avenues are scores of well-preserved and meticulously maintained houses that represent virtually every period in the storied history of the city. For example, the William S. Gaskins House, located at 702 East Front Street, is a handsome late-Victorian dwelling. It was constructed in 1885 by William Gaskins, whose ghost continues to dwell within.

Gaskins was a master carpenter who worked for a time for the Atlantic and North Carolina Railroad. His talents were well utilized in the construction of his two-and-a-half-story residence, which is one of the few surviving structures in New Bern crafted in the Italian Villa design.

About a hundred years after the house was built, the ghost of William S. Gaskins began making frequent appearances in the dwelling. In the late 1980s, the Fox family—Billy; his wife, Diane; and their two teenage children, Tere and Thomas—rented the house. Gaskins's ghostly presence was first noticed when doors began to mysteriously open and close on the second floor while the entire family was on the first floor. Conversely, when everyone was upstairs, kitchen cabinets slammed open and shut.

Billy Fox gave these phantom sounds little thought, owing to the drafty nature of the century-old house. But when pennies—very old pennies—began to mysteriously appear in the fireplace, the family started to wonder what was going on. According to Diane, the pennies, which were found on a number of occasions, could not have fallen out of the chimney, since it had recently undergone a complete renovation.

Things were to get stranger. About two o'clock one morning, Billy woke up in his upstairs bedroom and saw a light outside the room. Reckoning that one of the children had neglected to turn off the hall light, he arose and walked out to attend to it. But no electric light was burning. Instead, Billy saw a transparent figure standing by the banister. It was the apparition of a man in his sixties attired in gray work clothing, weighing around

170 pounds, and standing six feet tall. For almost ten seconds, the ghost stood there. Then it simply disappeared. Though shocked by the ghostly encounter, Billy was not frightened. He later described his experience as rather calm and peaceful. It had appeared that the ghost was on its way downstairs.

Cognizant that his revelation might be greeted with ridicule, Billy nevertheless decided to relate it to the owner of the house, since he was curious to ascertain the identity of the ghost. His landlord listened with great interest, then proceeded to do some research. Old-timers in New Bern who knew William Gaskins recalled that he often wore work clothes with suspenders. In their estimation, Billy's description of the ghost exactly matched their memory of Mr. Gaskins.

Other family members also sensed the ghost's presence. While watching television alone in the house, Thomas observed an unusual blur of light on several occasions. During a stay in the house, Diane's brother noticed that a number of items, including a box of cereal and a bunch of bananas, were mysteriously moved when no other human was in the house. And then there was Mercedes, the family's Lhasa apso. Animals are usually afraid of ghosts. However, Mercedes could often be seen in the upstairs hall, her tail wagging while she gazed down the staircase as if someone were coming to greet her.

All things considered, the ghost of William Gaskins has turned out to be a friendly, generous spirit. His periodic small gifts left in the fireplace have amounted to a handful of pennies dating from the late eighteenth and early nineteenth centuries. Perhaps the spirit of the old carpenter has left those ghostly presents as a token of his appreciation for the care that has been given to his architectural masterpiece. Ah, if only all haunted houses were so lucky!

Bewitched in Currituck

There is but a hairline between truth and superstition.

A. W. Tozer

Owing to its unusual geographic features and its location in the far northeastern corner of the state, Currituck County has long been known as "the Lost Province" of North Carolina. Despite its current state of relative isolation, Currituck, organized as a precinct in 1681, is one of the oldest political subdivisions of North Carolina. Accordingly, it was the stage on which some of our earliest colonial history was written.

Like many of the other Europeans who became the first permanent settlers of the Carolina colony, early Currituck residents maintained a strong belief in the supernatural. When he traveled extensively through the colony in the first decade of the eighteenth century, John Lawson, the first resident historian of North Carolina, was appalled by the "Thoughts of Spirits" that prevailed among the settlers. He fretted that stories of "Hobgoblins and Bugbears" were being told to the children of the Carolina province. In his famous journal, he made the following observation: "Their idle Tales of Fairies, and Witches, make such impressions on our tender years, that at Maturity, we carry Pigmies' Souls in Giants' Bodies, and ever after, are thereby so much deprived of Reason, and unmanned, as never Masters of half the Bravery Nature designed for us."

Toward the end of the seventeenth century, the fear of witches was very real in Currituck. By 1697, it reached the point of hysteria when a local woman, Susannah Evans, was arrested and brought before the General Court of Oyer and Terminer of the Albemarle. According to the witchcraft charges lodged against her, she, "by the institution of the devil . . . on or about the twenty-fifth day of July last past, the body of Deborah Bourthier . . . devilishly and maliciously bewitch[ed], and by the assistance of the devil, afflict[ed] with mortal pains, the body of the said Deborah departed this life. And also did diabolically and maliciously bewitch several other of her majesty's liege subjects."

After hearing the evidence against Evans, the grand jury ruled that the facts presented would not sustain a conviction for witchcraft. Cornelius Jones, a sea captain, served as foreman of the grand jury. Very much aware of the witch hunts and related executions that had recently taken place in Salem, Massachusetts, Captain Jones used his knowledge and powers of persuasion to convince his fellow jurors to dismiss the charges, in hopes of averting the panic so prevalent in New England.

Nonetheless, the witch scare already had a firm hold in Currituck. News of the unusual trials and public executions of witches in the North spread across the border from the ports of tidewater Virginia, where sea traders called almost every day. A second witchcraft case from Currituck soon made its way to the court. In the papers filed against Martha Richardson, it was avowed that the woman did "devillishly and maliciously Bewitch and by ye assistance of the Devil afflict the Body of William

Parker." Fortunately for the accused witch, the grand jury from the Evans case heard the evidence against Richardson. It ruled just as it had in the first case.

Over time, the legal proceedings involving witchcraft came to an end in Currituck, and the area avoided the garish executions of Salem. But don't think for a moment that the widespread local belief in witches ended when the legal accusations did.

On Knotts Island, the teardrop-shaped peninsula on the northern tip of the county, the early settlers—primarily Englishmen from London and Liverpool—had a strange encounter with a witch. The lasting effects of that incident can still be observed among descendants of those settlers.

In those days, rosemary was a much-desired herb for the seasoning of food. To the dismay of the new arrivals from Europe, there was no rosemary growing on Knotts Island. Then, early one morning, as the sun began to rise above the vast Atlantic, residents observed a tiny speck in the sea, making its way toward the old Currituck Inlet. The locals were mystified to see that it was a small boat plying the waters at significant speed without the aid of oars or sails. When the vessel made it to the Knotts Island shore, an old, eccentric woman known to all of the residents came ashore. Although the strange woman never divulged where she had been, the local gossip was that she had made a trip to England. With her, she brought a rosemary plant, which she promptly planted in the fertile soil.

As the days passed, the woman's odd behavior led the locals to suspect her of being a witch. Thereafter, the people of Knotts Island and other parts of Currituck County deemed the rosemary growing on the peninsula to be "witchy" and refused to consume it.

The witchcraft alarm that was sounded in Currituck over three hundred years ago is nothing more than a dusty page of the ancient history of this remote spit of land. Or is it? Just find some Currituckers whose roots are deeply entrenched and ask them about rosemary. Chances are their response will be this: "We don't use it because we don't like the taste."

The Evil That Will Not Die

There is a lurking fear that some things are not "meant to be known," that some inquiries are too dangerous for human minds to make.

Carl Sagan

From the Virginia line south to Bogue Banks on the central North Carolina coast, the famed Outer Banks stretch 175 miles in a semicircular arc. Hatteras Island, a slender, 56-mile-long barrier island shaped like a bent check mark, is strategically situated in the middle of this gentle geographic curve. In 1953, the island became part of Cape Hatteras National Seashore, the first such recreational area established by the federal government.

Hundreds of thousands of people from around the world flock to Hatteras Island each year to enjoy the miles of unspoiled Atlantic beach and the numerous historic sites. Chief among the attractions is the spectacular Cape Hatteras Lighthouse, the tallest lighthouse in America. Just south of the lighthouse, the landscape of Hatteras changes dramatically. Unlike most other portions of the island, much of the southern third is well forested. This area is known as Cape Hatteras Woods. Located near the southern end of the woods is the community of Frisco, one of the eight historic village enclaves on the island that were excluded from Cape Hatteras National Seashore.

Until a post office was established in the village in 1898, Frisco was known as Trent. It was here that one of the many haunting tales of the Outer Banks evolved in the early part of the nineteenth century. At the time, this part of Dare County belonged to Hyde County. It was inhabited by hardy islanders whose livelihood came primarily from fishing and livestock production. Cattle owners in Trent allowed their stock to wander the forest and the strand, which featured three significant sand dunes known as Stowe's Hills.

Absalum Clarke, who resided on the north side of Trent, was a wealthy man who owned one of the largest herds of livestock on Hatteras Island. At the other end of the village lived a hideous old woman by the name of Polly Poiner. Local gossip had it that she was a witch.

Because Clarke's animals were a valuable commodity, he paid great attention to their well-being. When numerous head of his livestock fell ill, Clarke was deeply concerned. Particularly troubling to him was the debilitating disease that struck his horses. They contracted lampas, a condition that causes the roof of the mouth to become inflamed and to swell. Workers were forced to put the unfortunate animals down.

There seemed to be no explanation for the sudden rash of livestock deaths until the bewildered Clarke overheard villagers discussing the strange behavior of the wretched Polly Poiner. While Clarke's horses and cows were dying in great pain, Polly's demonic laughter had been heard echoing from her hut. About the village, there was talk that the woman had put a curse on the animals.

Although Clarke was outraged, he elected—whether out of fear or doubt—to avoid a confrontation with Polly. But then his favorite stallion died mysteriously one day near the shore of Pamlico Sound. The site was not far from where an elderly woman had been seen looking for mussels. That woman was Polly Poiner, who was easily identified because she was badly stooped by rheumatism.

Clarke could stand it no longer. He dispatched a messenger with a dire warning for Polly: If she caused any further harm to his livestock, he would break her neck.

Polly was not intimidated by the threat. Before the sun went down that very day, Clarke's finest mare and her colt dropped dead. Once again, a witch-like cackle came from Polly's hovel at the edge of Trent.

In an uncontrollable rage, Clarke vowed he would dispose of the witch. Acting as if he were possessed, he made his way to her abode late one night. Polly was hard at work at her spinning wheel. Slipping inside without being detected, Clarke savagely attacked the vile woman and broke her neck.

The following day, two local fishermen found Polly's lifeless body. Although there were no eyewitnesses, all of the evidence pointed to Absalum Clarke. He was promptly arrested and jailed.

Clarke's trial was held on the shore of Lake Mattamuskeet in the mainland village of Lake Landing, then the seat of Hyde County. Circumstantial evidence proved to be sufficient to convict him. His subsequent execution is believed to have been the only public hanging in the history of the county.

A ballad was written about the strange case many years ago. It goes, in part,

> Oh that yaupon scrub and scraggly oak
> Quivered on the dunes when Polly spoke.

A madman turned a trick quite neat,
But the noose hung high in Mattamuskeet.

Back in Trent, the villagers carefully avoided the witch's former home.

Some years later, the property was acquired by an outsider who was unfamiliar with its history. When he learned of Polly's evil nature and strange powers, the man quickly sold the site to a resident of nearby Ocracoke Island. When the new owner began to till the soil in Trent, a frightening thing occurred. An old rope came slithering out of one of the furrows and suddenly raised itself at one end. Terrified at what he saw, the poor fellow screamed, "The old witch, she's still a-spinning!" He bolted away, leaving behind horse and plow, and never returned.

Since that time, this spot of Hatteras ground has been considered haunted. The few local folks who have mustered enough courage to cultivate the soil here have witnessed the same supernatural event: a rope that comes forth from the ground and loops itself into a hangman's noose!

That Certain Ghost

In *the white moonlight, where the willow waves,*
He halfway gallops among the graves—
A tiny ghost in the gloom and gleam,
Content to dwell where the dead men dream.

Frank L. Stanton

From our earliest history, the notion that a dead person can rise from the grave as an apparition of its former self has been popular in all parts of North Carolina. Accordingly, ghosts, like humans, appear in many shapes and sizes. And much like the deceased persons they represent, ghosts exhibit a variety of personalities. Three distinct ghostly behavioral patterns have been discerned in Tar Heel history: sad and melancholy; bright, happy, and mirthful; and malicious and deceptive.

Because most North Carolina ghosts spring from the tragic, violent, or untimely deaths of their real-life counterparts, they are rarely happy entities. Nevertheless, in this ghostly tale from Duplin County, the spirit that roams the historic City Cemetery in Faison exhibits the same happiness that a special little man once exuded.

In the second quarter of the nineteenth century, the Certain family emigrated from England to Southport (then known as Smithville), located at the mouth of the Cape Fear River. There, the family patriarch worked as a sea captain. Among the family members was little Cameron Certain, a boy of tender years when he arrived in North Carolina. Cameron matured into an outstanding young man who was blessed with exceptional musical talents. He became a renowned organ and piano teacher and was an accomplished dancer. But Cameron never grew in physical stature. He was a dwarf.

When North Carolina was drawn into the Civil War, Confederate forces seized Fort Johnston, the Federal military installation on the Southport waterfront. They established a training camp at the facility. Anxious to aid the cause of his adopted state, the tiny man volunteered to entertain the troops with his dancing and music.

In the initial wave of military units assigned to train at Fort Johnston were the Sampson Rangers, the first company organized in nearby Sampson County. Cameron Certain quickly developed close friendships with a number of the Sampson Rangers. When it came time for the gray-clad soldiers to head north to the battlefields of Virginia, the little musician decided to volunteer for duty in the Southern army. Alas! Because of his diminutive size, he could not pass the physical examination and was rejected as a soldier.

Not easily discouraged, the tiny fellow with an enormous heart volunteered and was accepted into the Confederate Hospital Corps. During the bloody fighting on the killing fields of Virginia during the Seven Days' Battles in the early summer of 1862, Cameron was a veritable angel of mercy. His dear friends from Sampson County and their Southern comrades suffered heavy casualties in their successful effort to keep the enemy away from the Confederate capital of Richmond. Amid the firestorm of bullets and exploding artillery shells, Hospital Corpsman Certain was in the thick of the action, rendering aid and comfort to the wounded and dying. Among the officers killed at the Battle of Gaines Mill on June 27, 1862, was Cameron's best friend from the Sampson Rangers, Lieutenant Colonel Franklin J. Faison.

When the war was over, the tiny hero returned home to eastern North Carolina and settled in Duplin County, where he resumed his career as a music teacher. For a time, he lived at Faison in the magnificent Faison-Williams House as the guest of Isham Faison, the wealthy planter and patriarch of the town that bears his family name.

His talents as a musician kept Cameron in great demand. He served as organist for Presbyterian churches in Faison and Goldsboro and provided music for numerous weddings and other special affairs. Indeed, for the remainder of the nineteenth century, the music of Cameron Certain brought great joy to many people.

Although Cameron was deeply religious, he was also fascinated by spiritualism and the paranormal. The little man claimed that he could communicate with the dead and that he saw ghosts. Probably his most interesting ghostly encounters were with the apparitions of two Yankee soldiers buried under one of the big magnolias on the lawn of the Faison-Williams House. Some say those spirits were part of the ghost troop of General Alfred Terry, who used the house as his headquarters during the waning days of the Civil War.

Despite his belief in the occult, Cameron was well respected by all who knew him. On occasion, he made light of the supernatural. One night, after reporting the appearance of a ghost on the grounds of St. Gabriel's Episcopal Church in Faison, Cameron was questioned about what kind of ghost he had encountered. His tongue-in-cheek response was that he reckoned it to be a holy ghost, since it manifested itself at a church.

Death took Cameron in 1901 near Warsaw, a town in western Duplin County. His request to be buried beside his Faison family friends in the ancient City Cemetery at Faison was honored. A horse-drawn hearse was loaded with the coffin bearing the body of the dwarf.

Somehow, perhaps through his dabbling in the paranormal, Cameron Certain seemed to have known he would return as a ghost. Strange things began to happen as the hearse made its way toward Faison. Something spooked the animals. In an instant, the hearse overturned and the coffin ended up in a ditch. After it was retrieved, Ed Mann, the proprietor of a store in the village of Turkey, agreed to keep it in his building overnight. Early the next morning, the cortege resumed its journey to Faison. But for many years thereafter, Mann's employees reported that they could hear coming from the store's attic the sounds of a piano playing beautiful classical melodies. There was no piano in the attic.

Following the interment of Cameron Certain in the cemetery filled with weathered tombstones and above-ground vaults, reports of bizarre occurrences began to circulate in Faison. When coon-hunting dogs made their way into the graveyard in search of their prey, their masters arrived to catch a fleeting glimpse of a tiny man nattily attired in a black velvet cloak near Cameron's grave. He disappeared into the opening of a nearby tree. Farm workers laboring in nearby fields at twilight have heard unexplainable sounds coming from the place where Cameron was laid to rest.

Should you care to make a nighttime visit to the City Cemetery in Faison, you might just encounter the strange apparition of a dwarf. But there's one thing for certain about the Certain ghost. He'll do you no harm, for he represents the life of a good little man who filled the world about him with music, dance, and happiness.

The Shriek of the Banshee

Extreme fear can neither fight nor fly.

William Shakespeare

One of the most terrifying figures of the supernatural world is the banshee, the messenger of death. After all, there is little more frightening than a symbol of death that imparts a dark and dire warning to its human witnesses: "As I am, so you shall be."

This female spirit is rarely seen. Rather, it is known for its haunting wail, which sends chills down the spines of all those who hear it. On the rare occasions when the banshee appears to the human eye, it takes the form of a young woman with flowing blond, white, or auburn hair. Most encounters with the harbinger of death occur in the late evening or early morning.

While the banshee is most often heard or seen at the birthplace of the person who is soon to die, it is also commonly found at or near well-known geographic landmarks, such as rock outcrops and rivers. Throughout history, most banshees have been associated with Scotland and Ireland. Few have been recorded in the United States. Even rarer is the banshee found in the annals of North Carolina folklore. Since Revolutionary War times, however, the banks of the Tar River near Tarboro, the seat of Edgecombe County, have been home to one of the most legendary of all banshees.

Most North Carolinians are familiar with the graphic scenes of flooded downtown Tarboro in the fall of 1999, after the Tar River poured out of its banks in the wake of the torrential rains occasioned by Hurricane Floyd. Almost twenty-two decades earlier, the Tar was less threatening, its dark, lazy waters controlled by a dam that disappeared long ago. Yet at that time, war was being waged in North Carolina. It was against this backdrop that the Tar River banshee made its first appearance.

Dave Warner, a native of England who had adopted the North Carolina colony as his home, operated a gristmill on a curve of the river below the dam. An avowed Patriot, he supported the cause of independence by providing grain and the use of his mill to the American army. From dawn until late into the night, the mill wheel turned continuously to produce badly needed foodstuffs for hungry Tar Heel soldiers.

Warner, a giant of a man, had black hair and a black beard that were often discolored by the copious flour that he produced. His massive arms and wrists enabled him to handle heavy sacks of grain all day long. There seemed to be no limit to his energy and his drive to win the war.

About high noon one hot, muggy day in August 1781, Warner was hard at work at his mill when he heard the sound of galloping horses. An informant suddenly appeared to warn him that the approaching horsemen were British troopers. "Close your mill and hide," the messenger implored. "The British know you for a rebel, and they will kill you."

Undaunted by the threat, Warner flexed his muscles and replied in a voice of defiance, "I'd rather stay and wring a British neck or two."

In one last attempt to dissuade him, the frightened courier admonished, "But you can't stay and fight a whole army single-handed."

In a calm, matter-of-fact manner, the burly mill owner responded, "I'll stay and be killed. What is my life?"

When the red-coated visitors arrived, Warner and the messenger were busy putting meal in sacks as the big wheel churned the river water. Six British soldiers bounded through the door, but the miller pretended he did not see them. To his young helper, he spoke words meant for the ears of the intruders: "Try to save every precious ounce of it, my lad, and we'll deliver it to General Greene. I hate to think of those British hogs eating a single mouthful of gruel made from America's corn."

Outraged by Warner's insolence, the soldiers savagely assaulted him. Although he fought with all his might, he could not overcome the five men who pinned him to the floor. Warner was not intimidated by their threat to drown him in the swirling waters of the Tar. He countered with an ominous warning: "Go ahead, go ahead, but if ye throw me into the river, ye British buzzards, the banshee will haunt ye the rest of your life, for the banshee lives here. When the moon is dark and the river's like black ink, and the mist is so thick ye can cut it with a knife, ye can see her with her yellow hair falling about her shoulders, flitting from shore to shore, crying like a loon. As sure as the stars are in the sky, if ye drown me, she'll get ye."

Taken aback by the miller's strange harangue, the Redcoats whispered among themselves. "Let's wait until the commander arrives," the tallest of them reasoned. "He will decide for us."

One of his compatriots quickly voiced agreement, but another, a rather large fellow with evil eyes, uttered a profanity and urged immediate action: "Why wait? We are sent on ahead to make the way safe. We'll get rid of this rebel before he makes trouble."

His words convinced two other soldiers to haul the miller down to the edge of the Tar. There, the Redcoats bound his arms and weighted his body with a heavy rock around his neck and another around his feet. Without hesitation, they then threw him into the dark water. As he sank, a bloodcurdling cry—the wail of a woman in pain—echoed along the banks of the river.

Overcome by fear, the soldiers watched in astonishment as a thick mist rose above the water. Before their very eyes, it took the shape of a woman with long hair, just as Dave had warned. Two of the men screamed in terror, "The banshee!" But the cruel soldier with the evil eyes was so frightened that he hurried back to the mill without saying a word.

The blackest kind of night had shrouded the river by the time the commanding officer and the main force of British soldiers arrived at the mill. They established an encampment along the river. While the enlisted men sat around fires near their tents, the officers enjoyed the relative comfort of the mill house.

A thin, yellow moon broke through the clouds and cast an eerie light over the entire campsite. Without warning, the stillness was broken by the unmistakable shriek of the banshee. All of the officers and most of the men rushed down to the river. Cowering inside their tent with their hands covering their ears were the soldiers who had taken part in the miller's murder. Once again, a misty cloud formed above the water and took the shape of a woman with flowing hair and a veil-covered face. All the while, the terrible wail reverberated up and down the river.

Filled with fear and guilt, the murderers related the events of the day to their commander. Disgusted by their conduct, he punished them by ordering them to remain at the mill, where they would work and be forced to endure the ear-piercing cries of the banshee.

After the army departed, the unfortunate men served out their sentence until one night when the banshee left the river and appeared in the doorway of the mill house. There, the soldiers witnessed a ghastly sight as the tall, misty figure flung back her veil and revealed a hideous face. Two of the men followed the banshee as it floated back in the direction of the Tar. At the river's edge, both stumbled and fell into the dark water, never to be heard from again.

As for the trooper with the evil eyes, he remained crouched in fear in a corner of the mill house. On that night, he went mad. He fled into the surrounding forest, where he called out the name of the miller. Within days, his lifeless body was found floating face up at the very spot in the Tar where he had sent Dave Warner to his death.

Since that time, August has remained a haunted month along the banks of the Tar River in Edgecombe County. And so this tale ends with a word to the wise: Avoid an August visit to the river, particularly on a moonlit night. Otherwise, you might hear an agonizing cry and see the ghostly form of the Tar River banshee—the portent of death itself.

Ghost of Deceit

The mysterious is always attractive. People will always follow a veil.

Bede Jarrett

Whether because of fear or because of rational business decisions, many of the historic haunted houses of North Carolina have been abandoned to the elements—and to the evil spirits that lurk there. One such dwelling is Stallings Place, located not far from Hobbsville in southern Gates County. Since the mid-1960s, the wooden, three-story plantation house has been devoid of human occupants. When the last owners took their leave, they left behind the ghost of a previous owner that had haunted the house and grounds since Reconstruction.

Whit Stallings owned the plantation when blue-jacketed Union soldiers scoured the Gates County countryside for spoils during the Civil War. "Old Man Whit," as he was called, was determined that neither his house nor his riches would fall into the hands of the invading enemy troops. Indeed, he went to extraordinary lengths to thwart the Union scavengers. But not long after the war, Old Man Whit died. To this day, his ghost lingers, apparently intent on protecting the property.

In its heyday, Stallings's house was a mansion. Constructed by artisans who used only the finest materials, it featured exquisitely carved moldings and woodwork in its interior. A long, cedar-lined driveway—now diminished by twentieth-century road construction—provided a picturesque setting for the grand estate. During the antebellum period, the mansion was the setting for grand affairs. Perhaps the most lavish of these was the wedding of one of Stallings's daughters. A magnificent reception that attracted the landed gentry from far and wide was held on the third floor.

Just when the house was built is unknown. However, by the time that hostilities between the North and South began in 1861, it was old. The Civil War spelled doom for the grand lifestyle to which Whit Stallings and his family had grown accustomed. As the war lengthened and intensified, Old Man Whit, cognizant of his well-deserved reputation as an affluent planter, reckoned that his home would be the target of Yankee raiders. Unwilling to part with his hard-earned wealth, he became obsessed with frustrating the attempts of Northern soldiers to rob him.

A shrewd fellow, Old Man Whit had converted his currency to gold in the early stages of the war. As soon as he learned that Yankee marauders were in the area, he quickly gathered his gold and the rest of his riches and buried everything at night in a secret spot, now believed to have been close to the mansion.

Word reached Stallings Place that some of the invading soldiers were making inquiries about Old Man Whit. Sly as a fox, he dressed himself in rags and appeared in public as a vagabond. Stallings was hauling a load of wood in a ramshackle wagon drawn by a scrawny mule when he encountered a party of would-be pillagers on the road to his house. In response to a question concerning the whereabouts of Whit Stallings, Old Man Whit said he knew no one by that name.

But no matter how hard he tried, the planter could not hold the plunderers at bay forever. One day, a Yankee soldier was reported missing. Gossip spread throughout the community that Stallings had killed him in the great hall of the mansion.

Once the war was over, Old Man Whit had little chance to restore his plantation to its former glory. Death came calling. The master of the estate took to the grave the location where his treasure was hidden.

New owners took possession of the estate. Rumors about the hidden riches circulated throughout the area, and eerie occurrences began to take place at the mansion. Often, when the entire household had retired for the night, the unmistakable sound of footsteps would disrupt the sleep of family members. Concerned that one of their number might be ill, the residents would arise, only to find nothing amiss. No sooner had they returned to their beds than the sounds would commence again. The mysterious footsteps were experienced at irregular intervals. The occupants speculated that the sounds were made by the ghost of Old Man Whit, who was either searching for or guarding the treasure.

Ever since Stallings's death, neighbors have reported lights burning in the rooms on the first floor. Before the house had electricity, a nearby farmer grew concerned when he saw lights on the lower level late one night. Fearful that his neighbor was ill, the man made his way to the plantation house to ascertain if he could be of assistance. When he reached the door, the visitor was astonished and frightened when the lights suddenly went out. Even more terrifying was the fact that every member of the family was fast asleep on the second floor.

Then there was the unsightly spot in the great hall. Most people familiar with the house believed that the stain marked the place where Old Man Whit murdered the Yankee soldier. Repeated efforts were made to remove the stain. Each time the floor was scrubbed with a strong lye solution, the spot would temporarily disappear. But when the area dried, the stain would always reappear, darker and more noticeable.

One of the last occupants of the house reported a strange incident with her house pet. Late one evening, the terrible wail of her dog awakened the lady. Turning on the light, she found the usually fearless canine cowering at her feet, shivering from fright. Its terror-filled eyes were fixed on the stairs. No intruder was found in the dwelling, but it took a considerable amount of time to pacify the animal.

Weeds and vines now threaten to make a jungle of the plantation that was once a showplace. Nature is set to reclaim the house, the ancillary buildings, and the grounds of Stallings Place. As far as anyone knows, the estate still holds the treasure hidden so long ago. But would-be fortune seekers should understand that their chances of recovering the riches are remote at best. After all, the clever ghost of Old Man Whit has been as successful in preserving the secret as was the flesh-and-blood Whit Stallings himself.

The Bear Creek Jack-O'-Lantern

The night has a thousand eyes.

F. W. Boudillon

What would Halloween be without the traditional jack-o'-lantern? Each fall, countless pumpkins are grown and sold throughout North Carolina for the express purpose of being carved into a decoration for the last day of October. Children of all ages revel in creating faces, whether happy or menacing, on their big, orange pumpkins. To provide an eerie effect, a candle is placed inside. Most Tar Heels consider the jack-o'-lantern synonymous with the fun and festivities of Halloween.

But throughout much of the history of North Carolina, the jack-o'-lantern was regarded as an evil entity. In the late eighteenth century, residents of the coastal plain reported sightings of bizarre lights in the dense, often impenetrable swamps. They referred to these frightening balls of light as jack-o'-lanterns— or simply as "Old Jack."

According to tradition, the jack-o'-lantern was born of hell when an unfortunate fellow by the name of Jack had the audacity to quarrel with the devil. As a result of the argument, Jack was transformed into a frightful demon and forced to float about the North Carolina countryside. Many Tar Heels came to fear the demonic Old Jack as much as they did Satan himself.

Experienced hunters and explorers disdained nighttime excursions into the swamps for fear of encountering the dreaded jack-o'-lantern. In the not-so-distant past, it was widely held that, once spotted, Old Jack would cast his spell on a person and lure him deep into the wilderness, where death awaited. On some occasions, the jack-o'-lantern would confuse deer hunters, causing them to mistakenly shoot a horse or other domesticated animal.

For as long as anyone can remember, Bear Creek, a tributary of the Neuse River that flows along the border of Greene and Wayne Counties, has been home to the sinister jack-o'-lantern. James Creech, who authored a history of Greene County in 1979, was a witness to the Bear Creek jack-o'-lantern while a teenager in the first half of the twentieth century.

His memorable encounter began on a hot, steamy night in late July. James gathered his fishing pole and headed for the creek and its chocolate-colored water teeming with fish. Clouds partially covered the moon, which made the evening unusually dark. To light his way to the creek bank, the young fisherman carried a kerosene lantern.

On that night, James was without human companionship. His usual fishing buddies could not accompany him because they were expected to work in the tobacco fields as soon as the morning sun began to rise. As he dropped his line into Bear Creek, insects buzzed about his face. The heavy, thick air made breathing difficult. The stillness was interrupted by the occasional croaking and splashing of bullfrogs.

Just as he was reaching the conclusion that the fish were not going to bite, James noticed a light in the distance. At first, he suspected that his friends had slipped off to join him once their parents had gone to bed. After collecting his fishing gear, he walked up the stream toward the light. In about a half-mile, he detected that the light was moving very slowly. He quickened his pace in an attempt to reach the other boys. As he closed in on the light, James shouted for his friends to wait for him.

Suddenly, the light ascended to a height of fifty feet, crossed Bear Creek, and floated slowly on the other side. James then knew that he was not chasing his friends. Instead, he had chanced upon the jack-o'-lantern. To the eyes of the amazed boy, the unusual light appeared to measure two feet wide and one foot deep. Its erratic movements continued until it paused near the edge of the forest. Then it rose higher into the sky and faded into the woods.

Fortunately for James Creech, Old Jack did not chase him that night. In the years since the incident, sightings of the Bear Creek jack-o'-lantern have diminished. Some scientists claim that the eerie light is nothing more than phosphorus created by rising swamp gas. As their theory goes, land reclamation along the creek has greatly reduced the amount of swamp acreage—and thus decreased the frequency of the light as well.

Rational explanations aside, visitors to the Bear Creek area of Greene County are well advised to keep a wary eye out for the unusual light that sometimes appears on dark nights. For, you see, this jack-o'-lantern is not the pleasing pumpkin that delights trick-or-treaters on All Hallows Eve.

The Strange Case of the Reverend Glendinning

As certain as the sun behind the Downs
And quite as plain to see, the Devil walks.

Sir John Betjeman

Throughout the annals of the Old North State, there have been many reports of the appearance of the devil. Two of the state's most enduring legends—the Devil's Tramping Ground and the mysterious hoof prints at Bath—have as their primary theme the presence of Satan on Tar Heel soil. From the coastal plain to the peaks of the Blue Ridge, numerous places and geographic landmarks bear the name of the devil. They were so named as a result of alleged visits by the original bad boy himself.

Even though these so-called devil haunts have an aura of unexplained mystery about them, most people are quick to discredit the notion that Satan ever physically walked the state. Nonetheless, there is one unusual written account of the devil's visits to North Carolina that may very well be true.

In his eighteenth-century autobiography, the Reverend William Glendinning, a Methodist minister from Brunswick County, Virginia, recorded a chilling account of his encounters with the devil in northeastern North Carolina during a six-month period in 1785 and 1786. His first reported visit from Satan took place in November 1785 while he was in Halifax County on a preaching mission. One evening while Glendinning was staying in the home of John Hargrove, some neighbors called on the minister. In the course of the ensuing conversation, the preacher shocked his audience by announcing that Lucifer would soon come calling at the Hargrove residence.

Almost as soon as he had made the startling revelation, a loud knock came at the front door. Upon opening it, the minister came face to face with the devil. "It was black as coal—his eyes and mouth as red as blood, and long white teeth gnashed together," Glendinning wrote. Startled by the horrid creature, the minister slammed the door, and the unwanted visitor left. About the same time, the wind blew and rain fell with an intensity never before experienced by the people in the Hargrove residence.

Over the winter that followed, the devil made appearances at the same home two or three nights every week. On the last such evening, Glendinning—staying with the family again—retired before the rest of the household. As the reverend lay in his bed, Satan peered in the window at him and said in a sarcastic tone, "O, that there was but mercy for the wretch that blasphemes the Holy One of Israel." Members of the Hargrove family who heard the voice thought it to be that of a man. But then the words were spoken again, and the minister informed his hosts of the speaker's identity. With that, Satan disappeared. Thereafter, he stayed away for several months, according to Glendinning.

The reverend's next encounter with the devil came during

daylight hours. Glendinning was in a field near the same house, having been driven there by the Hargrove children. At first, Satan began making his way toward the preacher and the young ones, but then he veered away toward a branch and disappeared. Glendinning subsequently recorded what is perhaps the most reliable description of the devil on North Carolina soil: "He appeared upward of five feet high, round the top of his head there seemed a ridge; some distance under the top of his head there seemed a bulk, like a body, but bigger than any person; about 15 or 18 inches from the ground there appeared something like legs, and under them feet; but no arms or thighs. The whole as black as any coal; only his mouth and eyes as red as blood. When he moved, it was an armful of chains rattling together." According to the minister, the Hargrove children acknowledged that they, too, saw the devil that day.

During the summer of 1786, Glendinning lived in a cabin on the farm of another family in the area. There, the devil resumed his visits with the reverend. On most occasions, Satan appeared in the early afternoon in the orchard near the cabin. In his autobiography, the minister chronicled that Lucifer would "shoot out of his head something like a horn of about six or eight inches high, above the top of his head." More often than not, the devil would then make his way to the roof of the cabin, which would inspire Glendinning to flee to the main farmhouse. In hot pursuit, the devil would enter the house and follow the minister from room to room. To drive the devil away, Glendinning would position himself near members of the family and shout the following words: "The Christian's God, rebuke thee, the God of Abraham, rebuke thee, God of the Prophets, banish thee, in the name of the Father, Son, and Holy Spirit, thou fallen angel disappear." Upon hearing Glendinning's words, the devil would begin trembling, and balls of fire would flame from his eyes. Each time the reverend used a biblical name, Satan would step back. Finally, he would vanish "as quick as lightning," in Glendinning's words. Some family members remarked that he often disappeared like a gust of wind.

Ultimately, these frightening encounters took a toll on the preacher, who reasoned that Lucifer had come to take him "bodily down into the pit." While three neighbor ladies were visiting him on one occasion, Glendinning revealed his fear that he might be taken to hell. When pressed on the issue, Mrs. Hargrove admitted that she had witnessed the devil come after the preacher.

In time, the strange visits from the master of hell reached an end, and the minister overcame the emotional trauma caused by the incidents. He continued his ministry in North Carolina and Virginia and extended it into Maryland and New York. A friend and close associate of Bishop Francis Asbury, Glendinning played an important role in the development of the Methodist Church in America.

As bizarre as Glendinning's account of his personal experiences with the devil is, it does appear to have some measure of credibility. Should you wish to read more of his account of when and where Satan walked in North Carolina, you can find a rare copy of the minister's autobiography—published in Philadelphia in 1795—in the library at the University of North Carolina at Chapel Hill.

Ghost of Invention

The graves stood tenantless and the sheeted dead
Did squeak and gibber.

William Shakespeare

Located on US 258 approximately a mile and a half north of historic Murfreesboro, the Gatling family cemetery is all that remains of the homestead that produced two brothers who were among the greatest inventors in North Carolina history. Buried within the iron fence here is James Henry Gatling (1816-1879), the older of the two imaginative and creative brothers. His more famous younger brother, Richard Jordan Gatling, was two years his junior.

The two boys and three other siblings grew up in relative affluence on a sizable plantation here. When Henry was eight, the family's log cabin home was replaced by what was called "the Great House," an immense, two-story mansion that stood nearby until it was dismantled in 1978.

From an early age, the Gatling brothers had an appreciation

for the outstanding mechanical skills of their father. Despite their common interest in the way things worked, the boys displayed different personalities. Henry was the dreamer and Richard the pragmatist.

In 1849, Richard was working as a store owner in his native county when he developed his first invention: the screw propeller for steam vessels. Unfortunately, when he arrived at the United States Patent Office in Washington with a model of his work, he was dismayed to learn that a patent for the same invention had been issued only days earlier. Unperturbed, Richard returned home and used his imaginative mind to produce other inventions. His seed-sowing machine—one of his many agricultural devices—was the first to receive a patent. In 1844, Richard moved to the Midwest, where he matured into one of the most talented inventors in American history. His most famous invention, a machine gun with a revolving cluster of barrels, revolutionized warfare after it was introduced in the 1860s. Unfortunately, the Gatling gun never achieved the purpose for which it was intended by its inventor. Richard once told friends back home in Murfreesboro, "It occurred to me if I could invent a machine—a gun—which could by its rapidity of fire, enable one man to do as much battle duty as a hundred, that it would, to a great extent, supersede the necessity of large armies, and consequently, exposure to battle and disease be greatly diminished."

While Richard was achieving international notoriety as an inventor, older brother Henry was busy back in Hertford County managing the family plantation. He expanded his father's varied business enterprises to include a winery and a fishery. Using his own creative genius, Henry invented several machines—a cotton thinner and a cotton stalk cutter among them—to make the plantation more profitable.

His business success translated into great personal wealth, which enabled Henry to spend time and money on his dream:

human flight. Several decades before the Wright brothers successfully conquered flight a bit farther east in North Carolina, Henry Gatling designed and attempted to fly a machine affectionately known to neighbors as "the Old Turkey Buzzard." According to a story in the *Raleigh Register* of March 19, 1872, Henry, a confirmed bachelor, was "at the old homestead, busy at work on a machine, that is destined at some future day to eclipse the famous gun, and fly triumphant over time, space, and water."

Tragically, before Henry could realize his great dream, he was savagely murdered by a deranged local man on the morning of September 2, 1879. Henry was feeding his hogs around sunrise when he was attacked. Reports indicate that he was wounded in the face by a shotgun blast and that his head was clubbed with a blunt object. When questioned about why he killed Henry Gatling, the murderer indicated he was angry because the victim had refused to give him a ride the day before the assault.

Following Henry's burial, the Gatling plantation was the site of three more grisly deaths within a fairly short span. First, a worker was killed when he was caught in the saws of a cotton gin. A few years later, the son of the plantation's new owner died when he fell into a peanut picker. Finally, an intoxicated black servant froze to death on the grounds.

In the aftermath of Henry's murder and the other deaths, reports of strange goings-on around the old homeplace began to circulate. Black farm workers reported being followed by a ghost that sometimes touched their shoulders. Local residents became convinced that the ghost was that of Richard Gatling, who had come home to avenge his brother's death.

Others have encountered the spirit of Henry himself. They believe that the restless soul walks the old plantation grounds to ensure that no further violence occurs there. Night after night, the ghost patrols the lane that led to the Great House. On one cold winter morning, Henry's ghost is said to have smashed a glass jar over the head of a plantation worker in the barn. Still another time, an opossum hunter heard Henry's voice coming from the cemetery. Other folks have seen Henry, as a headless horseman, ride up and down the mile-long Gatling Avenue near the spot where he was slain. With each ride comes the unmistakable sound of a panting horse and its pounding hooves.

Even though the Gatling homestead no longer stands, there are those who believe that Henry cannot rest in his grave. Should you venture up to the old plantation site on a dark night, don't be surprised to encounter the ghost of invention, who was robbed of his dream on a fateful September morning in 1879.

The Graveyard of the Atlantic

Fasten your seat belts, it's going to be a bumpy night.

Joseph Mankiewicz

After surviving a harrowing voyage through the waters off the North Carolina coast as a fifteen-year-old boy, Alexander Hamilton bestowed upon the place its enduring nickname: the Graveyard of the Atlantic. Throughout America's maritime history, no portion of the nation's coast has claimed more ships than this place where the cold Labrador Current from the Arctic violently collides with the warm Gulf Stream from the tropics to create a tempestuous sea. To make matters even worse, hazardous shoals—sandy fingers of death—lie hidden beneath the turbulent and treacherous waters.

The constantly shifting sands of the North Carolina coast will never disclose just how many ships and sailors have found their final resting place here. Historical research has verified the loss of more than two thousand vessels, and countless others have vanished without a trace.

As strange as it might seem, one of the freighters buried off the Tar Heel coast apparently returned as a phantom in 1976, thereby enabling the people aboard a foundering yacht to avoid the clutches of the Graveyard of the Atlantic. One stormy night that year, John Fielding, a respected engineer from San Francisco, was sailing up the North Carolina coast with his pregnant wife, Anna, and his seven-year-old daughter, Mary Jo, aboard the *Sea Quest*, a forty-one-foot sailing craft. The sea was rough and the wind high. Suddenly, Fielding heard a loud crash. He ran toward the bow to determine the source. And there it was: the cable extending to the end of the bowsprit had broken.

As the harried man scrambled to look for other damage, the savage winds snapped the main cable, which caused the mast to give way. Fielding knew that his boat was now in grave trouble. Fearing the worst, he rushed below deck to check for holes in the hull. Fortunately, the hold was yet watertight.

Fielding radioed a distress signal. His Mayday was picked up at the United States Coast Guard station at Ocracoke village. There, Chief Dan Robinson immediately ordered his crew to launch a rescue boat.

Aboard the *Sea Quest*, Fielding was both relieved that help was on the way and tormented by the thought that the Coast Guard might not make it in time. Violent waves and fierce winds were raking the sailboat, which was little more than a speck in a vast sea of darkness.

As the family watched and waited in fear, bright lights approached out of the storm. But it was not the Coast Guard; rather, it was a large freighter. The captain of the freighter brought his vessel alongside the yacht to survey the damage. Fielding could clearly read the name of the big ship on its bow and stern. Offers of assistance came from the deck of the freighter. As the ship's captain and Fielding talked by radio from boat to boat, the

Coast Guard was monitoring the conversation. Interrupting them, a Guardsman requested that Fielding obtain the exact location of the two vessels from the crew of the freighter. Fielding did so and relayed the information to the Coast Guard. Assured by Fielding that the rescue craft was very near, the captain got the freighter under way. In a short time, the Coast Guard boat arrived and took the Fielding family and its damaged boat to safety in the ancient port of Ocracoke.

At the Coast Guard station there, Fielding was asked the name of the freighter that had rendered assistance. The radio operator had picked up only Fielding's voice during the boat-to-boat interchange. When Fielding gave the name of the freighter and its captain, the Guardsmen looked as if they had seen a ghost. Actually, it was John Fielding and his family who had. For, you see, the freighter he encountered in the storm off Ocracoke had gone down years earlier under the command of the captain Fielding had identified. And so it was that a ghost ship deprived the infamous Graveyard of the Atlantic of another handful of victims.

JONES COUNTY

The Cove City Light

Give me a light that I might tread safely into the unknown.

Minnie Louise Haskins

Mysterious, unexplained lights have been observed and documented all over the world throughout the ages. Over the past 150 years, a disproportionate number of these spectral lights—usually blue balls or yellow spheres—have been reported in the United States. Alternately called ghost lights, spook lights, and earth lights, this supernatural phenomenon is formally known as ignis fatuus—"foolish fire"—probably in acknowledgment of the numerous unsuccessful attempts to capture, trap, or follow phantom lights.

From its aged mountains to its splendid shores, North Carolina boasts a multitude of ghost lights, including two of the world's most famous and most investigated—the Maco Light and the Brown Mountain Lights. Less familiar but equally fascinating and mysterious is the Cove City Light in Jones County. For 125 years, this eerie, orange, glowing ball has terrified, bewildered, and delighted travelers and hunters in eastern North Carolina.

If one dark night you should drive south on NC 41 from the village of Cove City toward Trenton, the seat of Jones County, located seven and a half miles distant, chances are great that you will encounter the Cove City Light along what is one of the straightest stretches of road in the entire state. Approximately a mile and a half into the trip, NC 41 enters Jones County from Craven County and penetrates the Great Dover Swamp, a vast, forbidding wilderness laced with creeks and branches flowing into the Trent River. It is at or near the highway bridges over these waterways that the Cove City Light is most often observed.

A number of eyewitness accounts have provided a similar description of the Jones County spook light. It is a glowing sphere, usually bright orange in color, that varies in size from as large as thirty feet in diameter to as small as a basketball. One of its most commonly observed tendencies is to follow vehicles as they pass along NC 41. Some motorists have endured the chilling experience of witnessing the light pass right through their cars.

Many local folks have come face to face with the Cove City Light on multiple occasions. One such individual is Duke Humphrey, who became fascinated with the ghost light in the winter of 1960-61 while on a double date with another teenage couple. Driving along NC 41 late one evening, the high-schoolers noticed an ominous light coming at them. From a distance, Humphrey made an initial observation: "It looked like headlights. You could see a long way down that road, and the light started as an orange light coming right up the middle of the road. I had been out there twenty times, I guess, looking for the light and had seen nothing but cars. This looked like cars." As the strange light drew closer, Humphrey was astonished that it was not a vehicle. "When it got to the point where the one light would always divide into two headlights, this one didn't," he noted. Instead, it turned out to be a solitary orange ball of light five feet in diameter. Traveling about three feet from the centerline of the highway, the ball flashed past Humphrey's automobile and floated down the road toward Trenton. He described the sensation experienced by the occupants of his vehicle: "We could feel it when it passed. It shook the car the way it would if a tractor trailer had passed, and the interior of the car heated up."

In the aftermath of that encounter, Humphrey gathered up three adventurous friends to go with him in pursuit of the light. Within a week, the heavily armed quartet was staked out in a car parked alongside NC 41 on a black winter's night. Their fearless leader recounted what happened on that occasion: "We saw it coming. It started like the cars, one light shining in the distance. As soon as it got closer, we could tell it was the light, so we hopped out and opened fire. It veered off the road over a field, stayed there for a minute, and took off as if nothing had happened."

Determined to bring the light down, the boys returned several weeks later. In addition to shotguns and rifles, their arsenal included a bow and arrows this time. Once again, the teenagers proved that the Cove City Light was truly a case of ignis fatuus. Humphrey later described the showdown this way: "This one was peculiar. Before, it had come down the road at a constant speed, never varying as it went past us. But this time, the speed was erratic. It seemed to almost stop and hover about 120 feet off the ground, almost over our heads." In an attempt to bring it down, Humphrey shot an arrow, which passed right through the light. A second arrow did likewise. These were the same arrows that Humphrey, an excellent archer, had used to kill a deer at a hundred yards. His compatriots likewise discharged their weapons to no effect. Humphrey was baffled. "There were four people shooting at it with guns, and I was using a bow," he recalled. "Nothing happened. It just drifted over our heads and then took off like always."

The following day, Humphrey returned to retrieve his arrows. He found only one of them, located some two hundred yards down the road. When it left his bow the night before, it had been as good as new. When he recovered the arrow, the varnished hardwood shaft was scorched, as if it had been exposed to intense heat.

From the time this bizarre light was first observed in the nineteenth century, many scientific explanations have been put forward: tectonic faults in the earth's crust; misinterpreted normal events such as auroras, fireflies, or swamp gas; man-made objects including vehicle lights and fireworks; deliberate hoaxes; alien craft; and secret government weapons from nearby military bases. None of these theories has proven satisfactory. But the belief that the spook light of Jones County is of supernatural origin has long held credence with local folks.

During hunting season long ago, bear hunters once sent their dogs into the swampy wilderness that borders what is now NC 41. Deep in the morass, the dogs gave chase to a mother bear and her cub. When the hunters came upon the cub, they killed it. The mother bear escaped into the swamp. Several days later, a lady and her infant were traveling in a buggy from Trenton to Cove City. At the moment the buggy crossed one of the bridges in the swamp, a large animal thought to be the she-bear lurched out of the woods, grabbed the child, and made off with it into the pocosin. The distraught mother sought assistance from the locals. A search party of hunters and woodsmen made its way into the often impenetrable wilderness. As daylight gave way to darkness, the overwrought woman joined the others carrying lanterns. After countless hours of roaming the accessible parts of the swamp without sign of the bear or the infant, the men called off the search. But the mother spent the rest of her life searching in vain for her baby. Her lantern, it is said, can still be seen along NC 41 on dark nights.

Now, before you scoff at that notion, be sure to observe the Watch For Bears signs as you travel NC 41 from Cove City to Trenton. Indeed, the wilderness along this lonely stretch is home to a healthy bear population. And one other thing. Local residents swear they can always hear the cry of a baby when the Cove City Light appears.

LENOIR COUNTY

Betty

The dead don't die. They long on and help.

D. H. Lawrence

The notion that the spirit of a loved one can make its presence known to the living is a commonly held belief that transcends the ages. A heartwarming incident that took place in Lenoir County several years before World War I lends credence to this time-honored conviction.

Located on SR 1324 at Falling Creek approximately seven miles west of Kinston, the Kennedy Home was established in 1912 by the Baptist Church as a farm for homeless children. By 1973, the complex had grown in size to more than twelve hundred acres.

Among the first youngsters admitted to the Kennedy Home when it opened its doors on June 5, 1914, was little A. C. Overton, whose parents had passed away earlier in the year. Prior to his arrival at the facility, the boy had lived at another Baptist orphanage, the Mills Home in Thomasville. There, he had learned to mend clothes worn by the children. In his private, lonely moments, A. C. longed for his deceased parents.

Despite his tender age, the little boy had a clear image of heaven and how it worked. A. C. was convinced that heaven was a big stable in the sky where good and upright persons went when they died. It was the youngster's belief that each inhabitant of heaven was given a white horse on which to ride back to earth to visit loved ones.

When A. C. arrived at the Kennedy Home, he was delighted to live on a farm where there were animals. Nonetheless, his daily life was mostly forlorn and gloomy, so badly did he miss his mother and father. Although his father had lived a respectable life as a fisherman, A. C. was not exactly sure he had made it to heaven. But as to his mother, the lad had no question. Night after night, he watched the sky for that special white horse from heaven.

The years passed. A. C. worked hard tending crops in the fields and doing other chores around the farm. On his fourteenth birthday, he was given a great honor: he was made a plowboy.

On the first day of his new assignment, the teenager reported to the large barn where the farm's twenty-five work teams were quartered. He passed stall after stall, admiring the large, dark horses as they pushed their heads forward for attention. At length, A. C. and the overseer reached the end of the barn, where a new stall had just been completed. Smiling, the kindly old man looked at his new plowboy and said, "Here you are, boy. Let's see if you can hitch her up."

A. C. could not believe what he saw. The horse assigned to work with him every day was the most magnificent, purest white horse he had ever laid eyes on. Without assistance, the boy carefully and gently hitched the animal to the plow. After the overseer gave A. C. instructions as to which field of corn he was to plow, the teenager started the horse in motion. Then, suddenly, he stopped, turned around, and respectfully posed a simple question: "Sir, what's her name?"

"Why, it's Betty," the man responded rather matter-of-factly.

As he headed into the field under a cloudless sky, A. C. looked up toward heaven with a beaming smile. The kind, loving lady who had given birth to him fourteen years earlier was Betty—Mrs. Betty Overton.

The Haunted Woods

Even the moon is frightened of me, frightened to death!
The whole world is frightened to death!

R. C. Sherriff

Should you travel east on US 64 from Williamston, the seat of Martin County, toward Jamesville, seven miles distant, your route will parallel the Roanoke River, which lies several miles to the north. Along most of this stretch, the highway is separated from the river by dense, forbidding swampland through which runs a dark-water tributary with a sinister name: Devils Gut Creek. A mile or so west of Jamesville, the desolate, swampy terrain on the north side of the highway gives way to a wooded area. But before you breathe a sigh of relief because of the change of scenery, be mindful that this forest has long been known as the Haunted Woods, thanks to the ghosts and other supernatural sights that have been experienced here.

From earliest times to the modern era, strange lights have

been observed in and about the Haunted Woods. Scientific minds have given the stock explanation for the weird radiance in an otherwise dark forest: gas from the nearby swamps. But local residents—the very people who have observed the lights over the centuries—have long held to a different theory. They believe the lights are the spirits of early North Carolina colonists who were murdered on the banks of the Roanoke by Indians in the first half of the eighteenth century. Those deaths—some of the most grisly ever recorded in Tar Heel history—are said to have given rise to the restless souls represented by the strange lights.

Whatever their cause, the lights of the Haunted Woods have frightened and mystified residents and visitors for many, many years. On a number of occasions, local hunters, some of them outstanding marksmen, have attempted to shoot the radiant balls. Their efforts have had no visible effect. Once, a pair of brothers attempted to hit the lights with gunfire. When they saw that their efforts were in vain, they hurried home, got some rope, and returned to the forest, where they proceeded to use a lariat when they again came face to face with the glowing lights. Try as they might, the men were unable to lasso the elusive spheres. All they could do was watch as the lights floated into the forest in the direction of the river.

Phantom animals and ghosts are also frequently observed in the Haunted Woods. For as long as anyone can remember, hunters and woodsmen have come upon dogs, cows, horses, and deer with a white, transparent appearance. Not even the best sharpshooter has ever been able to fell one of the spectral creatures.

In addition to the spirit lights and animal ghosts, the apparitions of humans have been encountered in the Haunted Woods, usually at one particular site. The Lynching Tree, alternately known as the Hanging Tree, is well entrenched in the lore of Martin County. An enormous oak with unusually long branches suitable for executions by rope, it was a well-known and ominous fixture in this supernatural forest until old age and the elements reduced it to nothing more than a stump.

In the middle portion of the nineteenth century, lynchings were not uncommon in Martin County and other parts of North Carolina. Instead of waiting for alleged criminals to receive official justice for their wrongdoing, vigilantes frequently took matters into their own hands. Sometimes, there was a hasty trial before a "hanging" judge and jury. But more often than not, the death penalty was pronounced upon the apprehension of the suspect. Many men breathed their last dangling from a rope attached to the Lynching Tree.

Not long after the lynchings commenced, reports of ghostly sightings at the tree began to spread throughout the countryside. One documented incident took place after a horse thief was hanged by a local mob. In the wake of his execution, area folks observed the ghost of a man hanging from the same limb used for the horse thief. According to eyewitnesses, the spectre cast a pale, silvery light.

Initially, the accounts of the ghost of the horse thief were met with ridicule. When the reports continued, three curious but disbelieving fellows paid a visit to the Lynching Tree. There, they saw it for themselves—a frightening, ghostly figure that emitted an unearthly light.

Word of the strange encounter by the trio of credible citizens created quite a stir. Next, a group of two dozen or more adventurous souls assembled to confront the ghost. Approximately one hundred yards from the tree, the ghost hunters selected five of their number to proceed forward. Upon seeing nothing out of the ordinary, the quintet summoned the others. As soon as the entire party was assembled around the oak, an apparition appeared from nowhere—a ghostly figure suspended from the tree. All who saw it were horrified. One man who was there that black night expressed the fear that gripped everyone: "The blood ran cold in my veins! A terrifying feeling came over me that I will never forget until my dying day." After a few minutes of silent observation, the horsemen fled the scene. Not a single member of the party was ever able to mount the courage to return to the site.

More than a century has passed since the last hanging took place in these woods. And even though the infamous Lynching Tree fell long ago, its ghosts linger. Balls of fiery light are still observed where it stood. Locals claim that the temperature at the site is several degrees higher than in the surrounding area. Human cries and sobs have been heard in this place where the noose ended many a life.

If on a dark, lonely summer night you happen to pass through the part of Martin County between Williamston and Jamesville, perhaps on your way to an Outer Banks vacation, don't stop, but do look and listen. You might just hear ghostly sounds above the din of frogs and crickets. And be warned that the eerie lights approaching your vehicle may not be fireflies. Rather, they may be the ghosts of these famed Haunted Woods.

The Fraternity of Death

So shalt thou feed on Death, that feeds on men,
And Death once dead, there's no more dying then.

William Shakespeare

No river in North Carolina is more steeped in history, tradition, romance, and mystery than the mighty Cape Fear. Thus, it is not surprising that the banks of the great waterway were the setting for one of the most bizarre unsolved mysteries in the history of the state.

The story unfolded in 1810, when a dozen young men from Wilmington, the great port of the Cape Fear, formed a fraternity. Its members, whose ages ranged from eighteen to twenty-five, were self-professed freethinkers. They openly rejected religion as an impediment to freedom of thoughts and ideas. Their reading list included works by Voltaire, an avowed atheist, and Thomas Paine, the American political theorist who postulated that Christianity was not a true religion.

Meetings of the fraternity were held at a cabin overlooking

the Cape Fear. On those occasions, the twelve brethren engaged in deep, penetrating discussions about their common beliefs. Most Wilmingtonians looked upon their activities with disdain, particularly after the men began to openly ridicule local citizens who attended church.

Contempt for the strange group reached its apex following an unusual supper held by the members. Ever anxious to mock organized religion, they took part in an imitation of the Last Supper at the cabin. One of their number was so sacrilegious as to assume the role of Jesus Christ. His fellow members portrayed the disciples. The men imbibed immense quantities of liquor during the supper. The event ended in a drunken melee.

If the club ever had a name, no one among the general public knew it. However, it could have aptly been called the Fraternity of Death, in light of the almost unbelievable sequence of deadly events that occurred following the Last Supper mockery. In the span of twelve months, nine of the young men died in a curious assortment of ways. The first to go fell dead as he was preparing for bed. A gunshot, believed to have been self-inflicted, felled the second member. Gossip was already widespread throughout Wilmington when a third brother met his demise in a fall from an upstairs window at his home. Next to die was an unfortunate fellow who borrowed a boat to go rowing in the Cape Fear; a day later, his lifeless body was discovered floating face down. His young age notwithstanding, the fifth member suffered a devastating stroke and died almost immediately. Members six and seven lost their lives when their buggy collided with a tree on an outing to nearby Wrightsville Sound.

As the mysterious string of deaths continued, the circumstances surrounding them grew more violent. The eighth resulted from a slashed throat. It seems that the young man was lashing a slave when the beaten man pulled a knife and slew him. Of all the deaths, the ninth and last was perhaps the most eerie. This club member was strolling past a downtown church one evening when the metal steeple suddenly and inexplicably fell. It struck the man in the head, killing him instantly.

For the trio of surviving members, enough was enough. They promptly disbanded their unholy alliance. The three lived to be old men.

Students of literature will readily find similarities between this tale of the macabre and "The Suicide Club," a story written by Robert Louis Stevenson for inclusion in *The New Arabian Nights*, published in 1882. There is some speculation that Stevenson heard of the strange story from North Carolina and loosely based his yarn on it.

Countless people have pondered the how and why of the mystifying happenings in New Hanover County in 1810 and 1811. Some believe that after their profane supper, the brothers entered into an unusual suicide pact. At each club meeting, they supposedly selected the next of their number to die. As the theory goes, the method of death was left entirely to the discretion of each member. Because the young men did not believe in an afterlife, they saw no wrong in suicide. An alternate theory holds that each of the nine was murdered by local citizens who were outraged by the club's unorthodox conduct and devilish activities. Divine providence has been cited as a third possible explanation for the weird events. Adherents of this theory believe that club members hastened their appearance before the throne of judgment by virtue of their extreme sacrilege.

Unanswered questions will long linger about this horrifying chapter of Cape Fear history. It will likely remain one of the great unsolved mysteries of the Old North State.

Tar Heel Giant

A Being, erect upon two legs, and bearing all the outward semblance of a man, and not of a monster . . .

Charles Dickens

Generations of youngsters have loved to fear the giant in the children's classic "Jack and the Beanstalk." For most Americans, young and old alike, giants are fictional characters confined to the pages of fairy tales. But in the first half of the nineteenth century, the people of northeastern North Carolina, southern Virginia, and eastern Tennessee were witness to a flesh-and-blood giant who may very well have been the largest human being ever to walk the face of the earth.

When he was born on a small farm near Rich Square in Northampton County in 1798, Mills (pronounced Miles) Darden was reportedly a normal-sized baby. Over the next fifty-eight years, however, he never ceased growing. At his death in 1857, the living giant weighed approximately 1,080 pounds and towered seven feet nine inches in height. Scientists have speculated that his enormous size was the result of a defective pituitary gland.

A farmer by trade, the Tar Heel goliath was by all accounts a gentle giant and a first-class citizen, in stark contrast to the infamous giants of literature. A deeply religious man, he was a devoted member of the local Baptist church. After his massive frame caused several pews to collapse, Darden worshiped with a prayer book in his hand while sprawled on a blanket in front of the pulpit.

In the field, the giant was a hard worker. It took at least three men to bind grain as Darden cut it. His extraordinary strength enabled him to single-handedly extricate from a mud hole a fully loaded wagon that a large group of men had been unable to budge. His booming voice could be heard all over the farm. Indeed, if atmospheric conditions were just right, Darden's words were audible up to eight miles away.

To sustain his hulking body, Darden ate copious quantities of food. As a teenager, he accepted a challenge from friends that he could not eat ten watermelons at one sitting. Taking a knife from his pocket, the massive adolescent proceeded to split open melon after melon. After fully devouring ten, he proceeded to eat another. Over the years, the man-mountain exhibited a voracious appetite. Newspaper accounts state that his "traditional" breakfast consisted of several dozen buttered biscuits, eighteen eggs, two pounds of bacon, and at least two quarts of coffee.

Darden had special requirements for his house, its furnishings, and his mode of transportation. Not only were the doors of his dwelling two feet taller than normal, they were also extra wide. Both his huge bed and his favorite reading chair were constructed of the sturdiest oak. On the rare occasions when he made an overnight visit, the considerate giant slept on the floor for fear of breaking a bed. No horse was large or strong enough to bear Darden. His only means of travel other than walking was an oxcart, specially built with heavy springs.

All of his clothing was either homemade or tailored. A tall, white hat the size of a beehive usually adorned his head. Some friends once had a fine suit of clothes made for Darden. When it was completed, three men, each weighing more than two hundred pounds, stood side by side, put on the coat, and fastened the buttons. It proved a good fit for the trio. Some years later, the ever-growing man required an even larger jacket. Thirteen yards of material were used to make it. The waist of his trousers measured seventy-two inches. If the cuffs were tied off, those trousers would hold ten bushels of corn.

When he was a young man, Darden moved just across the state line to the farm of his grandfather in southern Virginia. North Carolina's giant last roamed his native state in the late 1820s. Sometime around 1830, he moved his family to Tennessee, where he lived the last half of his life. Darden was last officially weighed before he left North Carolina. At that time, his poundage was recorded as 871.

Throughout his life, Darden took his great weight and height in stride. He attracted attention far and wide and received numerous offers to appear as the main attraction in carnivals and sideshows. Such efforts to exploit the giant were unsuccessful, because Darden was determined to live as normal a family life as possible. Until he was in his early fifties, he worked daily as a farmer and for a short time as a tavern keeper. But his uncontrollable growth ultimately made physical activity impossible and rendered him bedridden for the last two years of his life. During his final summers, slaves poured water over his immense body to provide some relief from the heat.

Darden married twice. He wed his first wife, Mary Jenkins (also a native of Northampton County), in 1820. Seven children were born to that marriage. Mary died in 1837, after which the giant took Tamesia Cooper as his second wife. Ironically, she weighed but ninety-nine pounds, so the couple presented a striking contrast. One account claims that Darden enjoyed picking up Tamesia with one finger. He was amused to hear her squeal when he held her high above his head. Records show that four children were born to Darden's second marriage. None of his offspring grew to be unusually large. Unfortunately, no photograph or artist's rendering of the giant is known to exist.

Death came to Mills Darden at his farm in Henderson County, Tennessee, on January 23, 1857. Physicians determined that he died of strangulation caused when the rolls of fat around his vocal cords closed his windpipe.

Removing his corpse from his house proved quite an ordeal. Finally, a section of wall had to be disassembled. Then a special casket had to be constructed to hold the mammoth body. According to contemporary accounts, the coffin was eight feet long and thirty-five inches deep. Upwards of five hundred feet of lumber and three pounds of nails were needed to complete its construction. Twenty-four yards of black velvet were used for the casket lining. Seventeen pallbearers strained to lift the body into the grave.

Should you care to visit the marked grave of the North Carolina giant listed in the *Guinness Book of World Records* as one of the largest men who ever lived, you can find it in a small family cemetery just off New Life Road some six miles southwest of Lexington, Tennessee.

Ghost Camp

The clang of arms is heard, and phantoms glide,
Unhappy ghosts in troops by moonlight seen.

William Wordsworth

Encompassing more than 151,000 acres and sprawling over 246 square miles in Onslow County, Camp Lejeune Marine Corps Base is one of the most important military installations in the world. This massive complex originated as a training camp for the First Marine Division on an 11,000-acre tract in the middle of a sandy pine forest just three months before the Japanese attack at Pearl Harbor. Originally known as New River Marine Base, it was renamed in late 1942 to honor Lieutenant General John Archer Lejeune (1867-1942), commander of the United States Marine Corps during World War I.

Today, the base stretches from its fourteen-mile Atlantic beachfront to Jacksonville, the seat of Onslow County, and beyond. Long considered the world's most complete amphibious marine training base, Camp Lejeune boasts fifty-four live-fire ranges, eighty-nine maneuver areas, thirty-three gun positions, and twenty-five tactical landing zones. For more than sixty years, American fighting forces have put the military skills learned here to good use in every corner of the world and in every war the country has fought during that time.

Over the years, hundreds of thousands of marines have endured long days and nights of grueling training in the isolated forests, sand flats, and beaches of the enormous complex. No doubt, duty in this wilderness can do strange things to a young marine's mind. Mysterious incidents have occurred within the deep recesses of Camp Lejeune. Two chilling stories recounted here offer a glimpse of the supernatural forces at work on the base.

On a cold November night in 1977, a platoon was on a training maneuver at Campsite 12 in one of the camp's countless pine forests. Just after midnight, the commander ordered four members of the platoon to move forward as a reconnaissance patrol. The remainder of the marines would follow an hour later.

After proceeding approximately a half-mile in a single-file line, the men in the patrol stopped abruptly in their tracks. Billy Joe, the point man, gave a hand signal that he had observed troop movement ahead. Believing that they were now involved in a war game, the four marines spread out, assumed their ambush positions, and watched for the enemy. Fifteen long minutes passed before any further movement was detected. This time, they saw something in the trees and also heard voices. Cognizant that no other forces were supposed to be training in the area at the time, the perplexed marines radioed their lieutenant and reported the activity. He confirmed their understanding that no other platoons were assigned to the locality. Then he ordered the four men to observe everything they could and to report their findings.

In order to determine the identity of the intruders, the patrol moved as close as possible without being detected. From their hiding spot, the four marines watched in disbelief. Before their very eyes, a large group of blue-coated Union soldiers went about the business of a Civil War campsite. Officers and men discussed the day's military operations against the Confederates while sentries did guard duty. Some of the guards passed within inches of the stunned marines. Smoke from cooking food wafted to the modern warriors as they took in the sights, sounds, and smells of the campsite of their counterparts from a different time and place. After an hour or so, the Yankee soldiers packed up and disappeared into the night. Soon after that, the marines radioed that all was clear. They were shortly joined by the remainder of the platoon. For fear of incurring the ridicule of their comrades and the wrath of their lieutenant, none of the four mentioned the bizarre events of the night.

Did four young marines on a routine reconnaissance patrol at Camp Lejeune suffer mass hallucination on a chilly night in late 1977? Maybe. But perhaps they saw a replay of the history that was written at the same spot 115 years earlier. More than two hundred soldiers of the 103rd New York camped in and around the Onslow County farm of Thomas Gillott in 1862.

Our second tale begins far away from Camp Lejeune. Bob, a member of the United States Marine Corps, was assigned to duty in London, England. During his free time, Bob spent pleasurable hours in historic Hyde Park, located near his quarters. On one occasion while he was sitting on a park bench, a man who looked to be about seventy years old asked if he might take a seat. Bob smiled and nodded.

Although the stranger possessed a pleasant manner, his physical appearance was suspect: he had shoulder-length gray hair; he wore a threadbare overcoat; and his feet were without shoes. Bob initially thought that the fellow was a drunk or a vagrant, but after they struck up a warm conversation, the marine was drawn to the man's deep, calming voice. He told Bob about the family he once had, the son he had left behind, and the places he had visited.

Suddenly, the old man stopped talking. When he spoke up again, it was to ask Bob for some spare change. As the stranger put it, he needed the money for the long journey upon which he was about to embark. Bob was only too happy to oblige him. In addition, he promised to buy the shoeless man some footwear.

As Bob reached into his pocket for some coins, his nameless friend put a hand on the marine's arm. Tears were rolling down the man's wrinkled face. Bob had to turn his head because he, too, was crying. Then he heard that soothing voice again: "There is no need to do this for me, Bobby. Your kindness is enough. We will meet again." Shocked by his words, Bob turned to look at the man, but he was nowhere to be found.

During the entire conversation, Bob had never once mentioned his name. Nor did he wear his name anywhere on his clothing. Even stranger was the fact that, as a child in Richmond, Virginia, he had been called Bobby by almost everyone, but most particularly by his father, who had died when the boy was six years old.

More than two years had passed since the odd encounter in Hyde Park when Bob found himself assigned to the First Battalion of the Sixth Marines at Camp Lejeune. While on maneuvers one day, Bob was shaving at his campsite in the base's wilderness. Nailed on a tree beside his shaving mirror was a picture of Mary Ann Mobley, an entertainer and former Miss America. Bob took the pinup with him everywhere he went.

There was absolutely no wind that day at the campsite, but the picture somehow blew off the tree. Bob stooped, picked it up, and rehung it. Again it fell, and again Bob stooped for it. Just as he prepared to stand up, he felt a gentle touch on his arm and heard a vaguely familiar voice call out, "Bobby!" Bob froze in his crouched position.

At that exact moment, an errant bullet fired from an M-1 rifle smashed into Bob's shaving mirror. Badly shaken but unhurt, the lucky marine hurried back to his tent to contemplate what had just transpired. Out of the blue, it came to him. The voice that had saved his life was that of the old man on the bench in Hyde Park. But who was it? Was it an angel? Bob knew—it was the ghost of his father.

Should you care to see Camp Lejeune, NC 172 will take you on a seventeen-mile course through the base that offers views of some of the vast wilderness where marines are trained for combat. Buried deep within these forests are some of the nation's greatest military secrets—and some of North Carolina's greatest supernatural mysteries as well.

A Brawl with the Devil

From his brimstone bed at break of day
A-walking the Devil is gone.
To look at his little snug farm of the world,
And see how his stock went on.

Robert Southey

Boaz Squires was not a famous Tar Heel to be found in the history books. But in Alliance, a small farming village in northern Pamlico County, the name is legendary. If something akin to a miracle occurs here, it is referred to as "a Boaz Squires deal." For in Boaz Squires, this part of coastal North Carolina had a flesh-and-blood wizard.

At an unknown time before the American Revolution, Boaz Squires immigrated to North Carolina from his native Scotland. He brought with him talents in magic and wizardry comparable to those of Michael Scott, the renowned Scottish folk hero. Boaz was one of the early settlers along the South Prong of the Bay River. Records indicate that his original patent encompassed land that stretched from the site of the former Alliance High School to the current county seat at Bayboro, several miles to the east.

Neighboring settlers took an immediate liking to the muscular young man. They quickly discerned that he possessed unusual powers, but they did not fear him. Rather, Boaz was admired because he represented the triumph of good over evil. Local folks were convinced that he held special powers over the minions of Satan.

To the delight of his neighbors, Boaz used his wizardry to build boats that were badly needed to transport local farm products, naval stores, seafood, and cattle to market. On one occasion, Boaz contracted with a neighbor to complete a boat for him in half a day. Even though his magic was well known throughout the area, no one believed that he could perform such a feat. After all, he had not a single helper. About midmorning, however, the sound of a crashing tree came from a forest owned by Boaz. Then neighbors heard such hammering and sawing that it appeared a work force of scores of men was on the job. Imagine the surprise of the local folk when at high noon they spotted a brand-new vessel afloat on the river. Sitting on board in a relaxed position and whistling a tune of contentment was none other than Boaz Squires.

How was it, the neighbors wondered, that Boaz was able to do the impossible—to construct a large boat in a single morning? To find an answer, some of the wizard's friends watched from a distance one day as Boaz went to work in the woods. They saw him lay his axes at the base of the tree he intended to harvest. He then placed saws, mallets, and other implements where they would be needed. And then it happened. In an instant, countless demons appeared and went to work crafting the project. Satisfied that the imps were on task, Boaz retired to more leisurely pursuits.

Area residents claimed that their wizard bravely battled the devil himself on more than one night. Maybe the Prince of Darkness sought these confrontations because Boaz used his demons like slaves. Whatever the reason, Boaz was sometimes taken away from his evening meal by a knock at his door. After the wizard was called outside, the unmistakable sound of fisticuffs could be heard. At length, Boaz, exhibiting a few scratches and bruises, would reenter the house, dust off his hands as a sign of victory, and resume his supper.

People in these parts grew confident that the devil had met his match. Yet Old Scratch held a card up his sleeve. Boaz had brought with him from Scotland an ancient black chest. Upon his arrival in what is now Alliance, the wizard had issued a prohibition against opening the trunk. For three long years, Mrs. Squires obeyed her husband's edict. But one day, something or someone aroused her curiosity, and she broke into the chest. Out sprang two demons in the form of a pair of large, terrifying black cats. Boaz fell dead immediately. Thus ended the saga of one of the most unusual supernatural presences in North Carolina.

Or did it? Folks in Alliance can show you the grave of Boaz Squires. If you choose to visit the site on a fall morning, be on the lookout for the misty cloud that often boils up out of the grave. Some say that old Boaz and his good magic are still with us.

Death House

*Men fear death as children fear to go in the dark; and as
natural fear in children is increased with tales, so is the other.*

Francis Bacon

Along a lonely stretch of SR 1103 on the southern
tip of Pasquotank County near the shore of Albemarle Sound
stands the two-story Shannonhouse-Lister House. Constructed
around 1816 and now abandoned to the elements, the dwelling
is one of the most haunted places in North Carolina.

In the early part of the nineteenth century, Thomas Lynch
Shannonhouse and his wife, Elizabeth, settled in this land of
swamps, cypress trees laden with Spanish moss, and dark, murky
water. Here, on a spot of rich, fertile high ground, the prominent couple built an impressive Federal-style house. Fortunately,
they never knew that the house of their dreams would become
one of misery, death, and horror.

Over time, Thomas and Elizabeth became the proud and
happy parents of ten children. One of their sons, John, born in
the house in 1824, came into possession of the property after

the death of his parents. John's favorite among his own children was his pretty daughter, Ellanora. A happy child of great charm and poise, Ellanora was pleasantly surprised on her sixteenth birthday—August 7, 1866—with a very special present from her doting father. John gleefully watched as the apple of his eye mounted the spirited pony he had given her. Thereafter, day after day, week after week, Ellanora spent many a pleasurable hour riding her treasured animal about the estate.

But on a Sunday afternoon six weeks after that wonderful birthday, a tragedy occurred that forever transformed the happy home into a place of sadness, gloom, and loss. On that fateful day, the teenager was critically injured when she was thrown from her pony.

For two days, Ellanora—her grief-stricken parents ever present at her bedside—clung to life, but there was no hope for her. Her heartbroken father was holding his precious daughter when she looked at him and whispered ever so softly, "But Father, I can't die so young." With those tender words, she closed her eyes forever.

In an instant, John's sorrow and grief changed to bitterness and anger. Before he left his dear Ellanora to the cold clutches of death on that night of September 20, 1866, he cried out in anguish a curse: "My most cherished possession has been taken from me. I hope all who inhabit this house may know the pangs of death which so pained me!"

From almost the very time that those words were uttered until the Shannonhouse-Lister House was abandoned in the second half of the twentieth century, at least one member of every family who lived in the home died there. Soon after Ellanora's death, the Shannonhouse family moved away, and the dwelling was acquired by Ephraim M. Stanton. Two of his small children promptly contracted diphtheria and died. In 1870, Stanton conveyed the house to a local farmer, Elisha Lister. As time passed, three of Lister's children died of disease in the house.

At the time of each such death, it was claimed by the inhabitants that a vague presence pervaded the house. For example, one of the subsequent deaths involved a farm laborer who fell victim to consumption. Just before he died in an upstairs bedroom, he spoke of seeing a girl riding down the road on a white horse. But no horse or rider had gone down the dead-end road the entire day.

In 1909, Elisha Lister's cousin was visiting the house when he died suddenly while sitting on the front porch. According to an eyewitness, he "suddenly pointed to the road, unable to speak, clutched his chest, and died instantly."

In 1923, three years after the Markham family moved into the house, Mrs. Markham was swinging on the front porch with her infant son. As she gazed down the road, she observed someone dressed in shimmering white atop a white horse. After receiving no response to the greeting she called out, Mrs. Markham walked into the yard with her child in her arms, only to see the horse and rider vanish before her very eyes. The next day, her baby fell ill. In a week, he was dead. Family members who were in the house when the tiny child passed away noted that the walls in the rear part of the parlor emitted a cracking sound. When the infant breathed his last, the strange noise abruptly ended.

In the late 1930s, the Markham family quickly moved from the house when another son grew ill. He survived, but the unfortunate families that followed suffered deaths. From time to time, the owners rented the house to families who were unaware of its dark history. None of the tenants stayed very long. One family moved out in the middle of the night. The young daughter of another tenant family reported that she was awakened one night by the sound of footsteps in the hall. Her bedroom door swung open. Suddenly, she felt the presence of someone at the foot of her bed. The terrified girl screamed and turned on the light, only to find nothing there. Other tenants reported hearing strange noises in an upstairs bedroom—the very room where those haunting words were spoken by John Shannonhouse so many years ago.

The last death took place in the house in 1969. Since that time, it has stood deserted, as no family is brave enough to challenge the curse that has brought sadness to so many. Perhaps, then, it is best that the house should forever remain empty, save for the restless spirits of a teenager and her pony.

Aunt Nora

An hour among the ghosts will do no harm.

Edwin Arlington Robinson

After some people pass away, their ghosts are said to linger at the homes to which they were so attached during their lifetimes. One such place is Poplar Grove Plantation, located on US 17 at Scotts Hill, approximately eight miles north of Wilmington. Should you happen to drive past the magnificent plantation manor house late at night, be sure to look for a mysterious glow emanating from one of the front rooms after all the lights have been extinguished. This spooky illumination is associated with Poplar Grove's resident ghost—the spirit of Aunt Nora Frazier Foy.

From 1795 until it was sold to Poplar Grove Foundation, Inc., a nonprofit corporation, in 1971, the majestic Greek Revival mansion was owned by six generations of the Foy family. James Foy, Jr., the son of a Revolutionary War Patriot, established the plantation. It once stretched from Topsail Sound to what is now US 17, encompassing more than 835 acres. Joseph Mumford Foy constructed the multistory frame mansion in 1850 to replace the original plantation house, which had burned a year earlier. Wood used in the house was hand-hewn and pegged, and the bricks in the foundation and chimney were made on the grounds.

Situated among stately oaks draped with Spanish moss, the mansion is listed on the National Register of Historic Places. It and the adjacent fifteen acres were opened to the public by the foundation in 1980. Tours of the exquisite dwelling and its dependencies offer a glimpse of what plantation life was like in the antebellum South. Visitors are treated to magnificent interior furnishings and exhibits that depict the plantation as it was in the early and middle years of the nineteenth century.

During your tour of this historic gem, you will come face to face with the portrait of Aunt Nora. If you look closely at her painting, you will probably reach the uneasy conclusion—as have most visitors—that her eyes are staring back at you. Perhaps it's because the eyes are tinted blue in a sepia print. But perhaps it's more than that.

Nora Frazier Foy was the grande dame of Poplar Grove from the time she came here as the young bride of Joseph Foy in 1871 until she died in the mansion in 1923. A colorful character, Aunt Nora enjoyed jokes, pranks, and smoking her pipe. For a time, she served as the local postmistress.

If you ask a member of the plantation staff about Aunt Nora, chances are he or she will tell you that her spirit is playful. Workers in the basement restaurant have experienced myriad supernatural occurrences before and after business hours. When no patrons were on the premises, phantom footsteps and slamming doors have been heard. Commodes have suddenly flushed in empty restrooms. Music from an unknown source has enveloped the restaurant. Cooks have witnessed every pot and pan in the kitchen fly off the hooks and crash to the floor in one thunderous fall. Managers of the restaurant have been spooked by some of the weird happenings and vexed by others. Late one night as a female employee worked in the office, she was terrified when the pages of a notepad on her desk slowly began to riffle. On more than one occasion, the manager has locked the place tight at the close of business, making sure that the stoves and lights were turned off, only to have the first employee arrive the following day to discover the lights burning and the stoves hot.

Bizarre events have occurred on the upper floors as well. One day when no other human was in the house, something kept picking up the extension telephone while a manager was on the line in another part of the mansion. Another time, a tour director was alone in an upstairs room when she saw an old wooden cradle suddenly begin rocking without being touched or blown by the wind. Then it stopped instantly.

Betty Taylor, a surviving member of the Foy family, has personally experienced some of the unusual goings-on in the house. After numerous problems with the burglar alarm, she marched upstairs one night to tell the spirit of her ancestor to stop putting out the cat at night, because it set off the alarm. There have been no further problems with it since that time.

According to Taylor, the resident ghost may not be that of Aunt Nora. Rather, she believes it to be another member of the family, a person killed in the Civil War. At least one employee agrees. Referring to the portrait of Aunt Nora, that employee said, "I don't believe [the ghost is] Nora. You just look at those eyes and let them look back at you, and you tell me she doesn't have a place in heaven."

But most people seem to believe that Nora's ghost still lives at Poplar Grove.

A special windowpane in the house bears the names of Nora and her husband, etched there on their wedding day. More than a hundred years after that event, a gentleman was making his way to his automobile after an evening meal at the plantation restaurant when he heard the sound of galloping hooves. To his surprise, a fabulous carriage drawn by two magnificent white horses was traveling up the tree-lined avenue. As it drew near, he saw that it bore a man and woman dressed in formal clothing from an earlier age. In an instant, the carriage disappeared without a trace, except for the hoof prints of its horses in the driveway. Was this a vision of the arrival of Joseph Mumford Foy and Nora Frazier Foy on their wedding day? No one can be sure. But it appears certain that once Poplar Grove became Aunt Nora's home, she never wanted to leave. And just maybe she hasn't!

The Ghost with Permanent Roots

In solitude
What happiness, who can enjoy alone,
Or all enjoying, what contentment find?

John Milton

A shallow, muddy bottom near the mouth of the Yeopim River at Drummonds Point on the upper waters of Albemarle Sound is all that remains of the island home of the first permanent white settler in North Carolina. Nathaniel Batts, an intrepid hunter and trapper from Virginia, acquired the island that bears his name on September 24, 1660. When Batts put down his roots here, he meant to stay. And stay he did, for it is said that the ghost of the first permanent Tar Heel can still be seen swooping down over what was once Batts Island.

Among the Chowanoke Indians who resided in this part of the Albemarle when Batts arrived, the uninhabited island was known as Kalola—a reference to the flocks of seagulls that flew above the spit of sand. In 1696, a deed recorded in the Chowan precinct documented the sale of the twenty-seven-acre island, which by that time was called Batts Grave. On the Moseley map of 1733 and the Collett map of 1770, the island was shown by the same name. Around the middle of the eighteenth century, it was said to have been as large as forty acres. But over the succeeding two centuries, river and sound erosion significantly reduced the size of the island. In the early part of the twentieth century, fishermen used the remaining portion as a camp. By the 1930s, only one acre remained above water. A hurricane that ventured into Perquimans County in the 1950s covered all that remained. Nonetheless, the spirit of Nathaniel Batts still lingers here.

Batts was a living legend among the settlers who followed him from Virginia into the Albemarle. His fearless nature and his local influence led those admirers to honor him with an unofficial title: Captain Nathaniel Batts, governor of Roanoke.

Batts, however, did not take any particular pleasure in the company of his fellow white settlers. Perhaps that was why he had fled Virginia. At any rate, he chose to associate with, and adopt many of the customs of, the Chowanoke Indians, who inhabited mainland Perquimans County. The Chowanokes admired Batts for his athletic physique and his outdoorsmanship. They invited him to accompany them on their hunting parties. Over time, he traded his European dress for that of the Chowanokes. And even though Batts Island was by then a veritable Eden of bountiful gardens and orchards, Nathaniel chose to live with his Indian friends in their mainland villages.

There was one Indian who attracted his special attention. Her name was Kickowanna, and she was the breathtakingly beautiful daughter of Chief Kilcocanen. She fell in love with Batts at first sight. But there was a rival for her affection. Chief Pamunky of the Chasamonpeaks in tidewater Virginia longed to have Kickowanna in marriage. When the lovely, young maiden with raven-black hair spurned his offer and openly pronounced her love for Batts, the jilted chieftain put his braves on the warpath. In the ensuing conflict between the Chowanokes and the Chasamonpeaks, Chief Kilcocanen had no better warrior than Nathaniel Batts. Conspicuous in combat because of his valor and battlefield prowess, Batts won enduring fame when he engaged Chief Pamunky in a hand-to-hand showdown. Pamunky went down after being sliced by Batts's claymore. Had the chief not begged for his life, the "governor of Roanoke" would have pummeled him to death with his club.

As a reward for his heroics, Batts was adopted as a member of the Chowanoke tribe and was given the name of Secotan, or "Great White Eagle." Thereafter, no tribal council, harvest celebration, or war dance took place without him. When the calumet—the pipe of peace—was smoked, the largest pipe was always given to Secotan.

As for the lovers, Kickowanna and Secotan married and settled down to a life of wedded bliss. The two often shared their hopes and dreams by the campfire that illuminated the dark Albemarle skies. On one such occasion, Kickowanna confided a great secret: when her father, Chief Kilcocanen, breathed no more, Secotan would be his successor. In preparation for that day, the Indian princess lavished ornaments and a fancy headdress on her husband.

Nathaniel Batts never lost his fondness for his little island paradise. From time to time, he would retire to his cabin there. On one such occasion, Kickowanna, lonely for the companionship of her husband, set out in her canoe to join him. As she paddled across Albemarle Sound, the bright afternoon sun was suddenly covered by dark, ugly, forbidding clouds. A torrential rain began to fall; thunder cracked; lightning streaked the sky; a savage wind blew; large waves gathered in the sound. Finally, a swell capsized the canoe, and the pretty Kickowanna drowned.

When her husband learned of the calamity, he was heartbroken. His life, his hopes, and his dreams were shattered. Nathaniel Batts never again left his island. When he died, he was buried there.

Although Batts Island now lies just under the surface of Albemarle Sound, seagulls still hover above and offer their lonely cries. On stormy afternoons, they are joined by the ghost of Nathaniel Batts, which sweeps up and down in its relentless search for the lost love of his life. Fishermen who ply these waters have heard a voice—a whisper in the wind—calling out, "Kickowanna, Kickowanna, Kickowanna." Indeed, the spirit of North Carolina's first permanent resident abides with us yet.

The Ghostly Light of Everlasting Love

Death—the last sleep? No, it is the final awakening.

Walter Scott

Romanticists have always maintained that true love never dies. That love can survive death and manifest itself beyond the grave has long been a common theme in the world of the supernatural. A case in point is the ghostly light that has been observed along the railroad tracks near the Pitt County town of Pactolus for nearly a century. It may very well be a tangible symbol of everlasting love.

Pactolus, a small village on US 264 in eastern Pitt County, is an old place, having been settled around 1790 by a Greek schoolteacher. Because the fertile land in the area yielded prodigious quantities of crops, he chose to name the settlement after the Pactolus River in Asia Minor, which was known for its unusual sand flecked with gold.

Its proximity to the Tar River enabled Pactolus to prosper as an agricultural center during its first century of existence. A new boon came to the village in 1892, when the movement of crops by rail supplanted shipping by water. In that year, the final link of the Washington Branch Railroad was completed in Pactolus. Before the advent of the automobile, this rail line was an important source of passenger transportation.

East Carolina Teachers College (now East Carolina University) opened its doors in nearby Greenville in 1909. It boasted 174 students. Glenna, the principal female character in this story, was a student there when the school was in its infancy. After completing her studies, she returned to her home in Richmond, Virginia, where she pined for her fiancé. While attending East Carolina, she had met and fallen deeply in love with David, a handsome young fellow from Greenville.

After the couple was separated for a period of months, the day finally arrived when Glenna boarded the train in Richmond that would carry her to Pactolus. From there, she would take a short buggy ride to be reunited with her future husband. David, however, was intent on making the reunion even sooner and sweeter. On the afternoon of Glenna's planned arrival, he saddled his horse and rode out to Pactolus.

As fate would have it, the train from Richmond did not arrive on schedule. As David rode up and down the tracks anxiously awaiting Glenna, the sun set and darkness enveloped the landscape. David soon became disoriented in the unfamiliar countryside. Now, there would be no surprise. Glenna would not even know he had come to meet the train.

As bad as things were for David, they were about to take a turn for the worse. His horse had attracted the attention of two lawless men who were loitering nearby. Anxious to steal the animal, they attacked David as he slowly rode past. David was killed during the savage assault. His murderers disposed of his corpse by dumping it in some dense vegetation. While they were doing so, David's horse escaped.

That horse made its way back to Greenville several days later. When they saw the animal, David's folks and Glenna realized that something was terribly wrong. They searched and searched for David, but their efforts were in vain. Once the search was called off, the heartbroken Glenna returned to Richmond.

Not long after David's death, an eerie light began to appear along the railroad tracks where the young man had waited for the love of his life. At times, the light appeared high off the ground, as if it were the ghost of someone riding a horse. On other occasions, it was closer to the ground, as if the ghost were walking along the railroad tracks. No other plausible explanation for the phantom light being available, local folks reckoned that it was David's ghost.

Over the decades since the murder, the Pactolus Light has been observed on countless nights. The old railroad line was abandoned in recent times, but the ghostly light continues to make its appearance. Romantic couples as well as fraternities and sororities at East Carolina University often make their way from Greenville to see the strange phenomenon. They have discovered that visitors to the site must watch in silence, for if an attempt is made to investigate the light, it moves away very quickly. As the legend goes, the horse that David's ghost rides is spooked by the activity and gallops away.

For almost a century, the Pactolus Light has appeared near the very place where David disappeared. This old ghost is persistent, for poor David wants to make sure he's there when the train bearing his dear Glenna once again pulls in at Pactolus. After all, true love never dies.

Creepy Crossing

So many ghosts, and forms of fright,
Have started from their graves tonight.

Henry Wadsworth Longfellow

Throughout the state's history, bridges have been some of the most haunted places in North Carolina. Friar's Bridge, found deep within the cypress swamps of Sampson County, is one such place. A bridge has been located here over Six Runs Creek since colonial times. The modern span crosses a wide expanse of swamp on the Old Warsaw-Clinton Road (SR 1919) approximately six miles east of Clinton, the seat of Sampson County.

It was in days of old when North Carolina was yet a colony that Friar's Bridge acquired its first haunt. On a deep, dark winter night, a coach carrying five passengers, including a newlywed couple, was making its way south toward Wilmington. As the stage made its approach to the wooden span, the driver and his team caught sight of the apparition of a woman dancing on the bridge timbers without making a sound. Terrified by the spectre, the horses panicked and sent the coach tumbling into the dark, icy waters of the swamp. The accident claimed the life of the young bride. After her body was located some distance downstream the following day, it was transported to Fayetteville for interment. Her grieving husband returned to his native England, where he joined the British navy. In the course of his service, he was lost at sea. No explanation of the strange vision that spooked the horses and driver at Friar's Bridge was ever put forward.

For a number of years after the accident, nothing unusual was reported at the bridge. Then came a night when a young married couple from the nearby village of Turkey had a frightening encounter. The man and woman were making their way home from a dance in Clinton when, from their buggy, they observed a young lady standing on Friar's Bridge. She appeared to be wearing a wedding gown. As the horse pulled the buggy closer to the bridge, it reacted in much the same manner as the horses that had caused the stagecoach to plunge into the swamp years earlier. Fortunately for the couple from Turkey, the husband was able to steady his horse and keep the buggy under control. In an instant, he leaped to the ground and pulled his lap robe over the steed's head. Then the man tried in vain to lead the hooded horse across the bridge. So terrified was the animal that it refused to move forward. Instead, it backed up and began to pull the buggy away from the bridge. Unnerved by the eerie presence and the abnormal behavior of the usually reliable horse, the couple returned to Clinton and stayed the night with friends. Unwilling to chance another meeting with the ghost at Friar's Bridge, they took a different, lengthier route home the following day.

As the story of the bizarre happenings at the bridge spread throughout the area, some local people greeted the reports with skepticism. One such doubter changed his mind after a personal experience at the haunted bridge. He was crossing the span one coal-black evening when he felt the sudden sensation that someone was breathing on his neck. Paralyzed with fear, the man was unable to move. When he mustered enough courage to steal a look behind him, he was mortified to see a young woman in white standing on the back of his carriage. Sharing the terror of its master, his horse galloped away at full speed and didn't stop until it reached the safety of a local farm.

In time, the ghost of the young bride was joined by another haunt. In the closing days of the Civil War, a black servant by the name of Radix was murdered nearby and was buried on the northeast side of the span. His slayers were believed to have been Union soldiers. Thereafter, people began to report a mysterious light in the swamp at the bridge. It would glow on rainy, foggy nights. Union cavalrymen who observed the light immediately turned back for fear that it was a party of Confederate scouts. Many years after the war, local residents claimed they had seen the ghost of the slain servant wandering among the Spanish moss-festooned cypress trees that thrive in the swampy morass.

Even today, daring travelers who choose to make the creepy crossing at Friar's Bridge at night should heed the time-honored warning to be on the lookout for the restless apparition of a bride who was deprived of wedded bliss and the ghostly light of a servant who was one of the many Tar Heel casualties of the Civil War.

The Lotus

Our ordinary minds demand an ordinary world and feel at ease only when they have explained and taken for granted the mysterious among which we have been given so short a license to breathe.

Llewelyn Powys

Rising in Hyde County, the Alligator River flows east and north to the Hyde County-Tyrrell County line, then flows along the entire length of Tyrrell County until it empties into Albemarle Sound. The famous Intracoastal Waterway follows the river for much of its length. On US 64 at the eastern end of Tyrrell County, motorists are afforded a splendid view of the majestic Alligator River from the nearly three-mile-long bridge that bears its name.

How the river received its rather ominous-sounding name is not known. Some contend it was so christened because alligators were found in its waters when the first white explorers and settlers came. However, it is doubtful that this picturesque river, its shores as primitive as they were when Sir Walter Raleigh's men first saw them in the sixteenth century, ever supported the reptiles in such quantity that geographers or local residents would have named the river after them. A more logical reason is apparent from a study of a North Carolina map: the river is shaped much like an alligator.

Whatever the origin of the name, the river and its undeveloped shoreline are about as wild as the fearsome creature itself. Mariners who dare to venture into the creeks feeding into the Alligator are treated to spectacular vistas of some of the most isolated, unspoiled land along the North Carolina coast.

Growing on the river near its junction with Albemarle Sound is the lotus, a beautiful tropical water lily. Flourishing here is a variety of the plant found nowhere else in the world except Egypt. Seeds from the lotus, if ingested by humans, are said to induce a dreamy languor and a state of forgetfulness.

Science has been unable to explain why this unusual variety of lotus thrives in this particular spot near the mouth of the great river. It is believed that the strange flowers were blooming when the first European explorers came upon the Alligator. Consequently, until a better theory comes along, an old Indian legend offers the best answer to the mystery.

Long before the arrival of white settlers, the Alligator and its environs were the domain of Indians from the Pungo tribe. Their chief, Wahoma, was a proud man who had one great, unfulfilled desire in life—a son. He prayed for a male child who might grow up to carry forward his position of power, responsibility, and honor.

In the twilight of Wahoma's life, it appeared that the prayers of the gray-haired chieftain were about to be answered. He learned that his young wife was with child. But when she delivered, the baby was a girl. Bitterly disappointed, Wahoma looked to the night sky as if to blame the god of the Pungos. At that instant, the brightest star he had ever seen caught his attention.

Convinced that the radiant heavenly body was a good sign, Wahoma reckoned that a new daughter was not so bad. After all, she would grow into a beautiful princess who would attend to all his needs. On the other hand, hunting, fishing, and fighting would have taken a son away from his father much of the time. But as hard as he tried to rationalize the situation, the chief could not completely satisfy himself that the birth of a daughter was a fortuitous event. Indicative of his doubt was the name he bestowed upon the child—Lotus, which meant "doubtful blessing."

More than a dozen years passed. Lotus matured into a young lady of striking physical beauty. Nonetheless, Wahoma's doubts were borne out by his daughter's indecent behavior. Lotus was a coquette who tantalized every young male in the tribe. They all fell for her, but she spurned each in turn, causing some of the most outstanding braves to either drown themselves in the river or run away to parts unknown.

It did not take long for the girl's flirtatious behavior to cause a tribal crisis. An assembly of elders was convened, at which one of the wise men observed, "A new star in the sky—cold, beautiful, dazzling, but of no earthly use. That was the sign of the gods." After a period of discussion and deliberation, the decision was made to bring Lotus before the tribal council to answer for her behavior. Her responses drew the ire of the men, who ordered her to be burned at the stake. Upon hearing the fatal pronouncement, tears welled in the eyes of the aged Wahoma. In an impassioned soliloquy to the council members, the weeping father entreated, "She is only a child. Forgive her this once. She has learned a lesson. She is my all." Out of respect and sympathy for the chief, the council agreed to spare Lotus.

Her new lease on life seemed to produce a positive change in her deportment—albeit a temporary one. Ultimately, she reverted to her former ways. The beginning of the end came when Lotus teased a young chief of the nearby Hatteras tribe. Upon being rejected by the alluring woman, he returned to his home on the Outer Banks and threw himself into the Atlantic.

A second trial was promptly convened. Once again, Lotus was condemned to death. Despite Wahoma's best efforts, the council would not commute the sentence. Lotus was tied to a stake erected near the river. As flames engulfed the body of the beautiful woman, her father, bent and withered by the passing of the years, watched helplessly. Her horrible screams and pitiful pleas for mercy pierced his very soul.

All attempts to lead Wahoma away from the scene were unsuccessful. The elders stayed at his side to offer words of consolation and comfort. He interrupted them to retell the story of the appearance of the brightest of all stars. They thought that he was mad when he told them to expect another sign.

While he spoke, the Alligator River suddenly began to rise, its dark waters dousing the embers of the pyre and sweeping up the ashes of Lotus. As the men watched in wonderment, the ashes swirling in the water blossomed into pale flowers. Turning to walk away, Wahoma spoke two words very softly: "The Lotus."

When the sun rose on the new day, every man, woman, and child in the village walked down to the river where the execution and the subsequent strange occurrence had taken place. Floating atop the water were thousands of lotus blossoms.

Thus, through the lovely flowers, the incomparable beauty of Chief Wahoma's daughter was preserved. However, so were her wanton ways. For, you see, the seed of the lotus blossom has the power to send young men to perdition, just as did the woman who bore the same name.

The Ghosts of Times Not Forgotten

*They'll soon forget their haunted nights; their cowed sub-
jection to the ghosts of friends who died . . .*

Siegfried Sassoon

Plymouth, the seat of Washington County, enjoys a splendid, picturesque setting on the Roanoke River. This historic town
gained prominence as a river port soon after its founding in the
late eighteenth century. Despite its age and its early prominence,
Plymouth boasts relatively few antebellum buildings. Because it
served as one of North Carolina's major battlegrounds during
the Civil War, the city suffered extensive damage. Soon after
Union forces gained a stronghold in eastern North Carolina in
early 1862, Plymouth was fortified into a veritable Gibraltar and
became a significant supply center for Union troops. In April
1864, the Confederates commanded by General Robert F. Hoke,
a bold, young Tar Heel, attacked and liberated the town in what
historians have concluded was the most complete and compe-
tent victory by Southern forces in North Carolina during the
war. But Plymouth paid a terrible price for the victory. Few struc-

tures survived the horrific artillery fire from both land and water during the three-day battle.

Perhaps the most distinctive antebellum building in town is the two-story Latham House, located at 311 East Main Street. This stately Greek Revival frame house was erected in 1850 for Charles Latham, a prominent attorney and politician. Many civilians in the town sought refuge in the basement of this dwelling while the Battle of Plymouth was being waged. Bullet holes—grim reminders of the war in which Americans killed Americans—can still be seen on the exterior of the house.

In recent times, the venerable house has been uninhabited, at least in human terms. On the other hand, it appears that ghosts have haunted the place almost from the time it was built.

Because of its location on a hill, the Latham House was built with an unusual feature for Plymouth: a basement. Of the five large rooms in the basement, the biggest is the former kitchen. It is here, in the window of the basement kitchen, that the oldest of the ghosts is represented by the flicker of a phantom candle.

The story behind this perpetual light unfolded in the decade before the Civil War. Economic woes forced Charles Latham to sell some of his field slaves. At the time, one of those slaves was in love with one of Latham's house servants. Unfortunately for the star-crossed lovers, the young girl's mother looked on the romance with great disfavor and forbade her daughter to see the field laborer. But when the elderly woman fell asleep, the maid would signal her beau with a burning candle in the basement window.

Then came the sad day when the slaves were loaded on a wagon for transport to their new owner, who lived across Albemarle Sound in Edenton. The weeping house servant trailed behind the wagon as long as she could, in order to capture one last glimpse of her true love. When she could no longer keep up, the young black man called out to her, "Don't forget to light the candle. I'll come for you."

Over the months of separation that followed, the girl clung to those words, faithfully putting a burning candle in the kitchen window every night. At length, the day came when the maid believed, albeit for a fleeting moment, that her dream had come true. On that occasion, the new owner of the slaves arrived from Edenton for a visit. Driving the carriage was one of the men who had labored in the fields alongside the girl's boyfriend. Upon seeing his face, she ran to the stable to inquire about her love.

Fate was not kind. The news was devastating. True to his word, the young man had attempted to keep his promise to come back for the girl. To that end, he had made a futile effort to swim the vast Albemarle. In the process, he had drowned.

Overcome with grief, the maid fled to the kitchen, where her candle was burning. Later, her lifeless body was found hanging from one of the beams in that room. She had voluntarily joined her boyfriend in death. But the light from her candle continues to flicker to this day.

On the upper level of the house is a bedroom that is also said to be haunted. The ghost that inhabits this room reflects the malevolent temperament of a former house guest.

James, a wealthy, young relative of the Latham family who came for a holiday visit in antebellum days, was a crude, callous fellow. Ever anxious to extend their hospitality, the Lathams assigned a personal valet to James. But rather than allowing the young black boy to sleep in the servants' quarters, James insisted that he sleep on the floor of the guest bedroom.

James's visit to Plymouth came at a time when the region was experiencing a bitter cold snap. Before James retired for the evening, the valet built a roaring fire in the bedroom fireplace. James slept in a big, comfortable bed covered with a cozy down comforter, while the valet made his bed on the wooden floor with but a wool blanket to cover him.

As the night wore on, icy winds blew outside. When the fire died out and the temperature in the room dropped significantly, James woke up in a rage. He shouted profanities at the valet for allowing the fire to burn out. He grabbed the boy's blanket and refused to permit him to go to the kitchen for some coal.

Once again, the two retired. James pulled both the comforter and the blanket tightly around his body. On the floor, the valet curled up in a ball as close as possible to the bed and gently tugged at the corner of James's covers. But James would not share, so the unfortunate boy was forced to endure the frigid air without any protection.

When James arose the following morning, he was incensed to find the valet on the floor beside the bed. He violently shook the boy, but his efforts were for naught. The boy had succumbed to the cold.

Soon afterward, people who spent the night in the bedroom began to report strange happenings. Their sleep was disturbed by a sudden, gentle pull on their bed coverings. To this day, folks say that the fretful moans and the chattering teeth of the dying valet can be heard in the house.

At present, the interior of the house is not open to the public. But if you happen to take a nighttime drive along Main Street in this historic waterfront town, be sure to look for the old Latham House. Its ghosts have left a light on for you.

The Cold Touch of Death

Let's talk of graves, of worms, of epitaphs.

William Shakespeare

From the coast to the mountains, thousands of historic cemeteries are scattered over the North Carolina landscape. For the timid at heart, a nighttime visit to one of these ancient burial grounds can be a harrowing experience, because many are said to be haunted by ghosts and spirits. On the other hand, a leisurely daytime stroll through an old graveyard can be a pleasurable walk back into history, for many of the weathered tombstones have fascinating stories behind them. Such is the case with two grave markers in a timeworn cemetery in Wayne County.

For seventeen-year-old Rachael Vinson, Christmas 1856 was a particularly happy time. Never before had she felt such splendor and anticipation. Indeed, she was filled with the unique excitement and ardor experienced only by those who are deeply in love. Her beau was an eligible local bachelor by the name of

George Deans, eight years her elder. Rachael dreamed about their beautiful wedding, scheduled for the fall harvest season in eastern North Carolina.

Alas, the nuptials never took place, for George soon revealed that he had become infatuated with another young lady. Poor Rachael was crushed. She lost all reason to live. Within weeks, her almost uncontrollable grief was replaced by sickness and fever. Her body was robbed of its vigor; her tender heart was broken; her gentle soul was stripped of its raison d'être. Just before her death, the jilted young lady called George to her bedside. She asked him to lean close to her. Then she whispered ever so softly, "I realize that I can never have you in this world, but I shall claim you in the next." On February 6, 1857, Rachael breathed her last.

A year passed, and another Christmas was at hand. At the height of the season's revelry, George and a group of his friends were walking home from a holiday party. Their route took them past the graveyard where Rachael had been buried earlier in the year. It rested on a high piece of ground above the winding road. From their vantage point, George and his compatriots observed a strange, fog-like mist rising from the bank above them. As the mist floated out of the cemetery toward them, it took on the appearance of the white, ghostly form of a woman.

Scared out of their wits, all the men save George fled the scene in great haste. For whatever reason, poor George could not move. He stood there as if made of stone, certain that the apparition was that of Rachael. He did not and could not say a word. Neither did the spectre. Then the ghostly form touched him! This phantom touch was made by a hand that was icy cold. It was literally the touch of death. Then, in an instant, the apparition vanished.

After a while, George's friends returned to look for him. They found him where they had left him—standing in a daze in the middle of the road opposite the cemetery. George looked as if he had seen a ghost.

When he awoke from a restless sleep the following morning, George was suffering from excruciating pain in the hand that had been touched by the apparition. Though he received immediate medical attention, the hand shriveled up over the course of the next few days and was useless for the rest of his life.

George Deans lived more than thirty years after the bizarre encounter with Rachael's ghost. There is no record that he ever married. After he died on June 9, 1889, his body was buried in the same cemetery that contained the grave of Rachael Vinson. Etched near the top of George's gravestone were two hands eternally clasped. Maybe that design represented the realization of Rachael's haunting deathbed utterance.

At George's death and for some time thereafter, folks in Wayne County remained skeptical of Rachael's ability to make good on her dying promise. And then it happened: some forty years after George was laid to rest, the likeness of Rachael's face mysteriously appeared on his grave marker. People who had seen a picture of the beautiful girl declared that the bizarre, life-size discoloration on the stone was the likeness of Rachael Vinson.

Deprived of the joy of promising "Till death do us part," Rachael made sure that death would keep her together with George forever.